Bound for Bodie

by

Ed Peoples

Dedication

This story is dedicated to Mama Ed,

as she was known in Crockett, CA

I carry her memory and her

zest for life in my heart

This is the first in the Clay Jameson series of novels by this author. This is also a newly released edition of the book, and is modified from the original to remove a trailer of another novel, *The Searching*, that was included after the main text of this book. That earlier book, *The Searching*, has been unpublished

Edited by: Nancy Costa-Matt, Thousand Oak, CA

Cover photo taken in Bodie
by the author

Table of Contents

Chapter 1

Morgan Williams had become an impatient man in his old age. Forty years of striving to maintain an empire had taken its toll. Trouble in the stock market in May was eating up his investments. His emotions were raw and his energy sapped. His current troubles had added a mood of depression and his once large erect frame was beginning to stoop at the shoulders, and his face was becoming pale and gaunt, and his thick shock of hair was greying more every day.

He had always been in charge and in control. He had met life head-on. It galled him now to feel that others were not at his beck and call, or that events beyond his control were impacting his life. His worst fear had come to pass: his daughter had either run off or been kidnapped.

He had gone to Oakland yesterday to hire a man whom he was told was the best detective west of the Mississippi. Clay Jameson was his name, and he had been considered by the Pinkerton agency as their best asset until last January when, for reasons unknown, he left Pinkerton and moved west to establish his own business.

The sign stenciled on the window said *Jameson and Cross, Detectives.* Williams was informed by a stylish looking young woman that the detectives were away, but that she would have Mr. Jameson meet him at Williams' office in Andersville the next morning. Williams waited now, in his own office, and occasionally spoke to someone in an adjoining office.

He paced back and forth in his office, occasionally looking down from a second story bay window onto Front Street, scanning the wharfs facing Carquinez Strait and the street below. Several of his schooners were tied up along the wharfs and men were coming and going up and down the street, but none were heading toward his door.

Then he saw him. It must be him. The man tied his horse to the rail in front of the building and walked confidently toward the door.

Williams noticed that the man was not large and tough looking, like he had hoped. He was in his mid-thirties, perhaps six feet with his boots on, and had a lean but solid frame. He seemed overly-dressed for the task that Williams would lay before him: fancy leather boots, dark brown twilled pants, white cotton shirt with a black string tie, a dark blue silk vest, a black three-quarter length coat, and a wide-brimmed Stetson hat with its high and round flat top, the one named by John Stetson the *Boss of the Plains*. A Colt Army revolver hung in a holster on his belt partially obscured by his coat. Something might have to be done about that, thought Williams. After all, this was 1893 and not many individuals walked around town openly carrying a handgun; and it might be too obvious for anyone who was worried about being followed.

Williams heard the man's boots on the stairs and then approaching the door. The man knocked.

"It's unlocked," bellowed Williams.

"Is that an invitation to enter?" The man responded in a firm but polite voice.

"Of course, it's an invitation to enter. What did you think I meant?" Bellowed Williams, with obvious sarcasm in his tone.

As Williams lumbered toward the door to open it, the man entered, closed the door a little harder than necessary, looked at Williams with a deadpan expression and said, "I am used to being met at the door and asked to come in. I don't care to be yelled at if we are planning to conduct business together." His pale blue eyes seemed to fade into slate blue-grey as his expression became more serious when he spoke.

Before Williams could respond, the man removed his hat, and stuck his hand out, walked toward Williams and smiled and said, "I'm Clay Jameson. I understand that you have need of my services."

Jameson looked around the office room while waiting for Williams to reply. It was a large rectangular room with mahogany walls, and a massive stone hearth nearly filled the outside wall. A six-inch-thick black oak timber mantel framed the hearth.

Jameson's reputation had been made during his tenure with the Pinkerton Detective Agency and had followed him out west when he left Pinkerton. Williams had learned what he could about the man.

Jameson was known to be of impeccable character and had worked hard to earn that reputation as a detective. He was somewhat of a legend. He was known to be a crack shot with a handgun or rifle, was equally capable of handling himself in any situation from bar room brawls to debutant balls, spoke three languages fluently, and was comfortable working with men or women from all walks of life.

There were also many tales about him, including him living with Paiute Indians; chasing the Hole-in-the-Wall gang; firing the final shots against the Dalton Gang's failed bank robbery last October; having fought for France against Bismarck's army; and having helped capture the outlaw Ned Kelly in Australia. He would have had to live three lives to accomplish all that, but then people do like a story.

Jameson had been briefed on Williams as well by his office staff and he had nosed around town talking to people and searching though current newspapers to learn what more he could about the kind of man Williams was before he met him. He learned that Williams was a man of questionable integrity, and was strong-willed and aggressive in his dealings with others, friend or foe. He openly displayed tremendous pride in his accomplishments. He was a man of great wealth and power in the area, but also a demanding and controlling man who expected others to do his bidding.

Williams was taken aback by the confrontive approach of Jameson, but he also realized that he had been blustery and rude when he knew that better manners were called for. He held out his hand and took that offered by Jameson. They shook hands firmly, each making sure that the other felt his strong grip.

"Sit down Mr. Jameson," said Williams. "I apologize for my abrupt manner. I've been on edge lately. And yes, I do have need of your services, if you're the right man for the job."

"And what would that job be, Mr. Williams?" Jameson asked.

Williams pulled his chair closer to the desk and hunched forward and said, "Do you know anything about me? Who I am?"

"Only what I've heard and read about you, Mr. Williams. You're a man of great wealth and influence, if that's what you mean, and you are also a man who has a problem or I wouldn't be here."

"I was born on the north western side of Wales, near the Irish sea," responded Williams. "A harsh and unforgiving land. I left home at age 14 and spent the next ten years at sea, then came to America and served briefly as a mate on steamers plying the Mississippi. My wife, Mary also came from northern Wales, from Llanbrynmair, to be exact. At age 18, she came to America with a group of twelve women in 1837, looking for a secure life, under the guidance of a Welsh Missionary. She soon secure employment in homes of influential families in the east. A hard life for her as well. Fortunately, we met four years later, fell immediately in love, and married. In May of 1849, we started west in a wagon train to California.

It was a long and hard trek across the plains and over the Sonora Pass; we then settled up in Tuolumne County, near Knights Ferry in 1850. We fought off the Paiute Indians from time to time and on occasion provided horses and food to Joaquin Murrieta and Three Finger Jack when they came by, just to avoid their wrath. We worked hard building up a large cattle business.

When the area became too hostile and dangerous because of the Indian wars, we moved our home and cattle away and founded a town near Fort Independence. We would have stayed there except that an old friend of my mine, Judge Anders, whom I met while traveling the Mississippi, owned 4,000 acres from a Spanish land grant *Rancho de la Prada* that stretched from Martinez west along the Straight to the point where the Straight widens into the bay. He offered to sell half of it to me at a next to nothing price. He practically begged me to buy it. The land offered promise and the location was better suited to expanding my business and closer to civilization so in 1864 we bought the acreage, drove the herd here and founded Andersville. We built a homestead and created what you see around today: cattle, shipping, warehousing, transportation, and we will soon have a large flour mill down in the flats west of here where the Straights narrow.

By 1877, the establishment of town of Andersville as a viable town was complete, as was our homestead. We built them together, as a family. My wife Mary and I and our children. We didn't beg, borrow, or steal anything. We got what we have by the sweat of our brows and the money in our pockets."

"You have much to be proud of, Mr. Williams, but does that explain why you need me?"

"No, it doesn't, but I tell you this as background so that you might better understand the position I'm in now. Life has been good, most of the time. I've been running the businesses for almost forty years. However, my oldest son Henry, who was primed to take over the business, was killed last year, drown somewhere out there in the straits while sailing. He always was reckless, a dare-devil when it came to sailing."

"Did they ever find him or the boat?"

"The boat was found two days later smashed up against the rocks on that island over by Marin County. The body never appeared. My second son, Hugh left home five years ago and went off to Venezuela to work in some mine for his uncle. We haven't heard from him in over three years. Broke his mother's heart."

"Excuse me, Mr. Williams, but are you getting to the point where you explain your need for my services?"

"Well, of course I am. Don't be so impatient. You need to understand my situation."

"And you need to understand, sir, that if you are going to be rude and demanding in our conversation, you will have to find someone else to hire." Jameson's tone was quiet, but cold and severe.

"Now see here..." and Williams caught himself and realized that he had been rude and demanding. That it was his usual manner in dealing with others. Anyway, he could see that Jameson wouldn't put up with it.

"I apologize again, Mr. Jameson. I have been beside myself with anger and resentment ever since our daughter ran off or was kidnapped. It is as if our lives have been put on hold. I don't mean to take it out on you."

"You say that your daughter ran off or was kidnapped. There is a difference, you know. I can\ understand the anger, but why the resentment?"

"We raised Megan with everything a girl could want. She had the best money could buy. We sent her off to Mills College in Oakland for four years to get the best education. Between school terms she would come home and work with me on the ranch and in the office. She was learning the business. Been a big help. With my sons gone, she was expecting to eventually take over. She had a real knack for business and for people. But I couldn't put a woman in charge, not with such responsibility. I expect her to marry well and bring the right kind of man to take over here. But now…Here, read this," Williams said, and he handed Jameson a folded piece of paper.

Jameson unfolded the paper and read:

Dear Mom and Dad,

I don't expect you to understand right now, but maybe at some point in the future you will forgive me. Zach and I love each other and we have eloped and have started our life together. I know you disapproved of Zach and wanted me to marry Clive Bristle, but I couldn't.

I won't tell you where we are going now, but I will write to you after we have settled and are standing on our own.

Your loving daughter, Megan

"So, we aren't talking about kidnapping any longer, are we Mr. Williams?"

"No, I guess not," Williams said reluctantly, "but that fellow, Zach, had a way about him. He wooed her and promised her a wonderful life, and she was just taken in by his fancy words."

"Mr. Williams, tell me about your daughter."

"Megan is young and naïve, as I have said. She is also a beautiful woman and her beauty and charm catch the eye of most men who see her. She's vulnerable, but she has spunk and tells me that she can take care of herself. She told us that she planned to teach at Andersville High

School when the new term starts, and then she just left. No goodbyes, no warning. She also is a stubborn, single minded, determined, and contrary person, and she knew we wouldn't let her go, if we could stop her."

"Stubborn, determined, contrary - humm. Where do you suppose she got those traits?" The tone of sarcasm did not fall on deaf ears.

"Alright, I know. She is a lot like me. No need to remind me of that now. The point is she is gone and I want her back."

"Does Mrs. Williams want her back as well?"

"Well of course she does. We both do."

It is just that throughout our conversation thus far you have referred to everyone as yours: *your* son drown, *your* son left, *your* daughter…I was just trying to get a feel for where you wife fit in to all of this."

"If my wife was here, I would have said *our*, but she is home and right now she is not involved in what I want. I want Megan home and I want that bum Zach out of her life. I want to hire you to find her and bring her home, and I don't care what it takes or what it cost.

"Well Mr. Williams, from the tone of her note to you, I would say that she left of her own accord, that she loves Zach, and that she doesn't want to be found."

"Well I don't think she is any condition to know her own mind. It's a romantic fling, an opportunity to shed the responsibilities she has carried in school and around here.

In two-months' time she will realize what she has done, but by then it will be too late."

"Too late for what, Mr. Williams?"

"Damn you. You can ask the most irritating questions. I should be asking the questions. Are you up to the task?"

"You mean that by then she will have become a used or tainted woman?"

" You have no right to speak to me about her like that," bellowed Williams. His face began turning red and his frame started to shake.

Jameson picked up his hat and tipped it toward Williams as a goodbye gesture, and he walked toward the office door.

"Wait a minute!" shouted Williams. "Where are you going?"

"I told you Mr. Williams that if you were going to rant and be demanding, you need to find someone else to hire. I won't put up with your bad temper. If you want to discuss a business proposition about me finding your daughter you will need to discuss everything in a calm and rational manner, and answer any questions I ask without becoming rude. I have better things to do than listen to you huff and puff. What will it be?"

Williams sat there quietly staring at Jameson for a moment, and then "OK, we'll do it your way, and I apologize, again." His body sagged and he folded his hands in his lap, as if he had given up the fight.

"That's better, and I think you will find that if we work together on this, we will be able to resolve your situation."

That seemed to calm Williams. The tension eased from his face and he leaned back in his chair and got comfortable.

"Tell me, Mr. Williams how long have Megan and Zach been friends and why would they feel the need to run off to get married?"

"Zachariah Colby Barnes is his birth name, and he grew up here, just a Megan has, and they attended the same schools, although Zach was two years ahead of her. I don't think they even said two words to each other while they were in school. They ran into each other at a Fourth of July dance down at the Grange two years ago, and got to dancing and talking, and seemed to hit it off, so she said.

He was between jobs and looking for work so I hired him to help with branding the young calves and shipping the older beef sold to the slaughter yards in South San Francisco. He and my ranch foreman, John Scully, butted heads from day one. Zach didn't like being told what to do, and Scully thought Zach was a lazy no account."

"How long did he work for you, Mr. Williams?"

"Only about six months. He was chatting up Megan at every opportunity, and never did come to Mrs. Williams and me to explain his intentions. I didn't think he showed us the proper respect. Scully complained about him almost daily, and finally said he would quit if I kept Zach on. So, I let him go.

I also told him not to come around Megan any more unless he asked our permission. Megan was furious, I know, and I think she met Zach on the sly at every opportunity when she wasn't away at school. It drove a wedge between us for a while, but then about two months ago, Megan seemed to change her attitude and stayed around the house. She even allowed the neighbor boy, Clive Bristle to call on her. I wanted her to marry Clive. He comes from a good family and would be just the kind of guy to run our ranch someday. That was just the lull before the storm. Mother and I came home late one afternoon from shopping in the city. We were gone all day and, in that time, Megan had packed some of her clothes and personal items and was gone. I immediately checked with Zach's parents and at the Consolidation Freight Company where Zach was then working. They had the same story. He just left. They thought maybe he had run off with Megan but weren't sure until finally Zach's mother confirmed it. We were the only ones upset by the situation. So, there you have it Mr. Jameson. Now will you find her for me?"

"I will take the job, and will do my best to find her, but there are no guarantees, you understand. I'll need to gather a lot more information and try to learn where they went; or at least which way they started. You also understand that if and when I do find her, or them, she might not want to come home. We will have to deal with that at the time. I'll have my office send you a contract which you will need to sign and return immediately. I think that time is of the essence here, so I'll begin today and assume that you will have signed the contract. We charge $50 per day for myself and the use of my horse, plus out of town expenses, which will apply in this case. I will require an advance of $350, payable before I begin work."

"You said you will begin working on the case today, but you require an advance before you begin work. I am not sure what all that means."

"It means that you need to pay me $350 before I leave your office today. I anticipate having immediate and on-going expenses for travel. I'll need a photograph of Megan, a recent one if you have it."

Williams sat slumped in his chair staring at Jameson for a long moment, as if he was looking for reassurance that this would end quickly and well. Finally, he took a wad of bills from a desk drawer and counted out $350 and handed it to Jameson. Jameson took out a receipt book from his coat pocket and entered the details of his hire and the amount of the advance. He handed it to Williams who laid it on his desk without looking at the print.

Williams took a photograph of Megan from his desk drawer and handed it to Jameson. "Remember," stated Williams, "I don't care what it takes or what it cost. I want her home, and I want him gone. I understand that you can handle the rough stuff if it comes along. Is that right?"

"I can handle it.   Before I get myself into a tight spot, I have already planned the way to get out of it."

"Like I said, Clay, I want Zach gone. I will pay a $500 bonus if you can assure me that he is gone for good."

"That I can't do, Mr. Williams. I don't make people disappear. I'll keep you posted on my progress. Good day to you sir."

"Good day, Mr. Jameson, and thank you. I look forward to hearing from you."

After Jameson left, Williams walked to the window and watched to be sure that Jameson had actually left the building. Then he went to a connecting door with a second office and opened it. Scully walked into the main office.

"I assume you heard all that, Scully?"

"I did, boss, and it sounded like he wasn't going to be much help even if he found her. He'd let her go with that dumb clod if she wanted to and he would not do anything about Zach. I told you, boss, that you should let me handle it. I'll bring her back whether she want to or not, and I will have no problem in making Zach disappear, for good."

"Where will you find her, Scully?

"Well, that's the problem. Who knows where she went?"

"That's the point, isn't it? Jameson is a trained detective and I think he can find her if anyone can. After he finds her, however, that is where you come in. I want you to follow him where ever he goes from now on. If he talks to anyone, find out what he learned. Stick with him like his shadow, and when the time comes, you'll know what to do."

"That might take days or even weeks, boss."

"It might. That's alright. Whatever it takes. Here is $200 for expenses. Take Rand with you. He'll follow orders and a second gun might come in handy. You bring my daughter home, and bring me proof that Zach is done, and there is a $500 bonus in it for you. Promise
Rand whatever you need to, and keep a close rein on him. He doesn't always think before he acts."

"You got it, boss. It's as good as done."

Scully stuffed the money in his shirt pocket, shook Williams' hand and strode out the door and down the stairs.

Rand met him at the street level. He was holding their horses. They talked briefly, and then rode away together.

Chapter 2

Clay Jameson was a very cautious man who trusted no one, and was a man who went to great lengths to be prepared and to stay ahead of whomever he encountered.

He had arrived an hour early at Williams' downtown office on the day of their scheduled meeting. He took a window seat at the dockside café located diagonally from the office window and waited and watched. At about 9:30 a.m., two riders pulled up to the rail in front of the office building. One was a rough looking burly man wearing an old brown felt wide-brimmed hat pulled down tightly over a mop of thick matted black hair.

His black leather vest bound his upper portion of his portly frame. He dismounted, handed the reins of his horse to the other man, a tall and gangly man who appeared to be Mexican. He wore a small brimmed sombrero and had a red bandana tied around his neck. They exchanged words briefly, and then the first man entered Williams' office. The other man left the area, taking both horses.

Within a few minutes two men appeared at the upstairs office bay window, and they scanned the street below as they talked.

Jameson left the café by the side door so as not to be seen from the front street where Williams might be looking. He mounted his horse, rode around the corner and tied up at the rail in front of Williams' office to keep his appointment.

There was nobody else in the office but Morgan Williams when Jameson entered for their appointment. Also, there was no sign that anyone had been there, although a light from an adjoining room shown under the door.

After Jameson left Williams, he rode off on his horse, but once out of sight he rode around in back of the warehouses and came out on Front Street right next to the café's side door. He entered the café and took the same window seat to again wait and watch. This time he ordered hash and fried eggs and black coffee and began reading a local newspaper that someone had left on the table.

The burly looking man came out of Williams' office after about ten minutes and was joined almost immediately by the Mexican. They talked briefly and the burly man patted his front pocket, as if to indicate he's *got it*.

As Jameson was watching the two men, the waiter brought his breakfast and noticed where Jameson was looking. "Oh, mister," offered the waiter, "I wouldn't mess with those two. They're bad medicine."

"Who are they?" asked Jameson.

"The big, crude looking guy is John Scully. He's the foreman at the Williams ranch, and the Mexican looking guy is a half-breed named Rand Gomez, a ranch hand. White mother and Mexican father. Story is that when he was fourteen, he killed his father, slashed his throat, for beating his mother, and when he was fifteen, he shot his mother for bedding with some sailor just come off a ship. Nobody could prove nothing, and if you ask me, nobody cared about what happened to them types. Like I say, they're bad medicine. When Mr. Williams wants something bad to happen, he sends them two."

"Thanks for the warning. You can bet that I'll keep my distance from those two. Good hash, by the way." Jameson added, after downing a fork full of his breakfast.

After breakfast, Jameson visited the parents of Zach Barnes. Their house was located at the end of Edward Avenue, a short street off the main road through town. It was a large house built in the second empire-style, with dormer windows in the front and sides of the upper story.
It appeared to have been newly painted a light green and trimmed in black.

Flowers and small scrubs were arranged in symmetrical fashion in the front yard. A middle-aged man and woman sat in matching wooden rockers on the wide front porch.

Jameson rode up to the front of the house, dismounted, and tied his horse at the rail in front. The man rose from his chair to greet Jameson and the woman sat up in her chair and smiled. They both appeared to be in their mid to late sixties, and both looked tired. He was tall and lean and she was short and pleasantly plump, as my grandmother used to say about certain women.

"What can we do for you, mister?" asked Mr. Barnes.

"Well, I'm hoping you can help me a whole lot. I assume that you are Mr. and Mrs. Barnes."

"Yes, we are. I'm Bob and this is Helen. And what might your name be?"

"My name is Jameson, Clay Jameson, Mr. Barnes. Is there some place where we could sit and talk for a few minutes?"

"That depends upon what you want to talk about."

"Oh, come on Bob. Ask the nice man up to the porch where we can sit and talk all he wants," interrupted Mrs. Barnes. "You sit down right here, young man," and she pointed to one of the wicker chairs on the deck. "I'll go get us some lemonade."

Mrs. Barnes soon returned with three glasses and a pitcher of cold lemonade and poured them each a glass. "Now, Mr. Jameson, is it?"

"Yes Ma'am."

"How can we help you?"

"I am here to discuss the where abouts of your son, Zach and Megan Williams."

Mr. Barnes quickly looked over at his wife, and she let her eyes fall to her glass of lemonade. Then he looked at Jameson with a scowl on his face and a tone of irritation in his voice. "Did Williams send you over here to snoop?"

"No, Mr. Barnes, I came over here to snoop all on my own. I need your help to prevent trouble for Megan and your son. I need to find them before someone else does."

"What do you mean, before someone else does?"

"I'll lay out the whole story and you can answer that for yourselves. Mr. Williams hired me to find his daughter and bring her home. He thinks her behavior was rash, that she was pressured by your son, and that she'll regret it later. He wants her home and Zach gone."

"You mean he wants Zach dead?"

"He never used the word *dead*, but I got the distinct impression that he wouldn't mind if that happened. I told him that I was not in the business of making people disappear. I also told him that I would look for Megan and if and when I found her, I would try to convince her to return home. If she didn't want to return, I wouldn't force her, and I would do whatever I could to help her and Zach, if they wanted my help."

"So, what did you mean when you said you wanted to find her before someone else does" What someone else?"

"Well, here's the problem. I saw Scully, Williams' ranch foreman, enter his office before I got there for our appointment and I am sure he was in the next room listening to the conversation between me and Mr. Williams. After I left Williams' office, I watched the doorway from the café across the street and I saw Scully come out of the office and meet with Rand Gomez for a few minutes. Scully patted his pocket as if to say to Rand, *I got it, or have it.* They rode off together. I am concerned that if I don't find Megan and Zach and warn them and protect them, Scully and Rand will find them.

Who knows what might happen then? I don't know what kind of a man your son is and whether he could or would fight Scully to protect Megan. Whatever happens, it won't be a pretty scene."

"Oh Bob, what are we going to do?" Asked Mrs. Barnes. She was obviously distressed, and she was forcing back tears.

Mr. Barnes reached his arm over and around her shoulders, trying to comfort her, and he said, "Now mother, this is not the time to worry. We've got to keep calm and help Mr. Jameson all we can."

Then Mr. Barnes looked toward Jameson and said, "We are church-going Baptists and had Zachariah in Sunday school and in church with us until he got old enough to know his own mind. He was assertive and stood up for himself when he was in the right, but he didn't take to violence. Even when he was in grade school, he wouldn't fight when the other boys teased him or took something of his. He'd yell at them and face them, but he just wouldn't fight them. Now, I don't know Mr. Jameson. I don't know what he would do if confronted by Scully."

"Does he have a gun of any sort?"

"No, not now. I bought him a shotgun once when he was young and we went out bird hunting. A flock of geese flew overhead and I yelled at him to shoot. He shot and hit two geese. They fell at his feet, dead and bloodied. He got a sickly pale look on his fact, threw the gun down, and heaved up his breakfast. Then he began crying and ran home. We never talked about that incident and he never touched that gun again. So, I don't know, Mr. Jameson. If you ask me, he had too much sin and damnation stuffed down his throat from that preacher at the First Baptist church. I just don't know what he'd do in a life or death situation, or a situation to defend Megan.

We'll just have to let that play out."

"Well, if you ask me, interjected Mrs. Barnes, "you placed high demands on him and he couldn't measure up. That church going has been good for him. While we think the world of Megan, I think that this marriage gave her a chance to escape. But I agree with Bob. We'll just have to let this play out and hope for the best. God will watch over him."

"No, Mrs. Barnes, I don't think that God is watching right now and we can't wait to see the end... That is why I need to find them. And there are things I need to know. Do you have a photograph of him? Can you tell me what he was wearing? How did they leave, on horseback, by wagon, or by boat? What can you tell me?"

Mrs. Barnes gave Jameson a photograph of Zach and told him what they knew. It seems that Zach and Megan were married here in the Barnes' house by the local Baptist minister just hours before they left.

"It was short wedding, but ever so sweet. They were so much in love," said Mrs. Barnes. "Zach had obtained a wagon from Consolidated Freightways, where he worked, and we gave him two horses, two Shire draft geldings for a team. They are eight years old, but they are strong, and smart, as horses go, and they have an easy-going temperament. They left Wednesday, June 23 on the 2:30 p.m. steamer from Martinez going to Sacramento. From there they were to going to Bodie and set up shop. A store to supply the gold miners with whatever goods they need, and Zach planned to include a repair shop as well. He's real good at fixing things."

"But Bodie," interrupted Jameson. How did they ever decide on Bodie?"

"Bob's brother, Harry Barnes has run a store in Aroura, Nevăda for over twenty years, and wrote often about how successful it was and how much more business there was for some energetic young man. Zach read that often enough and heard stories about Aroura from others that he decided he would move there. However, in his last letter, Harry said that the mines had played out in Aroura and that the town was a bust. He moved his store his store about seventeen miles west to the booming town of Bodie, California. Zach and Megan plan to join him in Bodie and then set up their own place."

"I've been to Aroura, Mr. and Mrs. Barnes. It's about sixty miles south of Lake Tahoe and located in the high desert, over 8,000 feet. In 1860 the population was about 100, and then gold was discovered. By 1863 the population had exceeded 5,000, mostly males. The town consisted of numerous houses, 20 stores, 12 hotels, 21 saloons, and 2 newspapers, and a dozen or more brothels where half the female population of white and Chinese women worked as prostitutes. It was a violent place where gunplay and killings were commonplace. If you want to read a good description of life there, read the book, *Roughing It*, by Mark Twain. I am glad your son and his wife aren't going there.

However, the town of Bodie is no better. Gold was discovered there in 1859 and at one time there were thirty gold mines in operation, and they used both cyanide and mercury in the processing, a deadly combination, as so many men learned to late. Both chemicals poison the organs of the body, as well as polluting the environment However, because of the demand for miners, the population there grew of about 10,000, making it the second largest city in California.

The Main Street was a mile long and every other building was a saloon. In addition to bar, there were numerous brothels, gambling halls, and opium dens.

It was a wild town, and rumor had it that there was a man killed almost every day.

A story goes that one little girl whose family was moving to Bodie, wrote in her diary: 'Goodbye God, I'm going to Bodie.'"

"Good Lord, Mr. Jameson. It sounds worse than Sodom and Gomorrah. None of us ever dreamed it was like that. How did my brother, Harry, ever want to live in places like Aroura or Bodie?"

"He probably found it was a good place to sell supplies to the miners and make a comfortable living However, Bodie started to decline in 1882 and the population dropped to 3000 inhabitants. I'm sure it's even less now. Aside from the violence, it is one of the coldest places to live in California. There is heavy snow and wind all winter and even in the summer months, the temperature can drop below freezing at night. I probably won't be able to convince Megan and Zach to come home, but I sure hope I can convince them to move somewhere where the conditions are bearable and a man can make a living without gunplay going on all around him."

"You'll find them, won't you, Mr. Jameson? You'll get 'em somewhere safe? Let the Lord go with you."

"I sure will, ma'am, I sure will. And I'll let you know how it went. And you folks stay here and say nothing, especially to Williams and his men. Do you understand, Mr. Barnes? Don't do anything or say anything and don't have any contact with Williams?"

"We understand, replied Mrs. Barns. "I know that Bob will be getting angry thinking about what all you've said, but I'll be sure he stays here."

"That's what I figured. That's why I said that. Mr. Barnes, will you stay away from Williams?"

"I'll try, Mr. Jameson. I'll try."

"Trying won't work, Mr. Barnes. I need a positive commitment. Will you stay away?"

"Okay. I will. Yes, I will."

Jameson left with the impression that Bob Barnes was a hardworking man who might demand that his son be a man, and the Mrs. Barnes believed that God was watching over it all. Otherwise, nice folks, living a simple life. Jameson hoped that he could bring Zach home to them.

Chapter 3

Clay Jameson tied his horse up to the rail in front of Consolidated Transportation. He had seen his friend and the owner, Bill Heck, earlier this morning and arranged to bed down there tonight on a cot in the tack room, then head out tomorrow in search of Zach and Megan.

He had always told folks that he had known Bill since Heck was a pup, and for the many who didn't understand the joke, he left them wondering, as if they had missed some great words of wisdom.

Clay Jameson and Bill Heck met on a trail drive about thirteen years earlier, pushing a herd of 2,000 longhorns from Texas to the Caldwell, Kansas stockyards. Twelve miles a day at best, and they brought them in with plenty of meat on their bones. Jameson was young and a little wild and Heck held him in check and taught him about trail riding, among other things.

They worked together on the trail and they drank together in towns along the way, and occasionally fought together. It was one of those life experiences that binds men together, as well, and they had become as close as two men allow.

The front door to Heck's business opened to a show room featuring two new wagons, several hand-tooled saddles, and an array of harnesses, along with one wall filled with work pants, shirts and hats. There was a wagon repair shop in the back of the store that also housed several used wagons for rent, along with a stable of both wagon and riding horses for sale or rent.

Heck looked up from the store counter as Jameson walked in.

"I was thinking about you after you left this morning. It's been a long time, but you still look just as ornery. What did Williams have to say?"

"At first he said his daughter had either run off or been kidnapped. But as you know, she eloped with your guy Zach. He wants his daughter to come home and he wants Barnes to disappear, but it's more complicated than that."

"Let's go back into my office and you can tell me all about it."

Jameson shared what he knew with Bill Heck, and they discussed what few options were open to satisfy Jameson's contractual obligation to Williams and the need to protect both Megan and Zach Barnes.

"I know why they chose to go to Bodie, but they have no idea what's in store for them. Mr. and Mrs. Barnes said you gave Zach a wagon and they gave them two horses. What sort of wagon was it?"

"Actually, I didn't give Zach a wagon. He's the kind of guy who can repair anything. I was boasting about him to one of my customers and he offered Zach an after-hours job of repairing three old wagons out at his ranch, and promised Zach his choice of the wagons if he could repair them. They were old and in bad shape. He worked there on his days off and I'd let Zach off early if we weren't busy so he could work on the wagons. It took him two months, but he fixed all three so as they were like new. My customer was both amazed and pleased and he not only gave Zach his choice of wagons, he gave him two $20 gold pieces as a bonus.

"So, what kind of wagon do Zach and Megan have?"

"Zach re-built a Rack-Bed Wagon, which he thought would be useful for traveling in mountainous terrain, as if he had been planning their trip all along. He installed ratchet style brakes with a manual foot lever, and added

---

wheel rub brakes as well. The wagon box measured thirty-eight inches wide and ten and one-half feet long and two feet high, with the driver's box in front and the seat mounted on two wide steel bar spring risers. The box and seat were re-built of poplar lumber and the gear and tongue of ash. A tool box area was located in the boot, in front of the driver's area. When Zach got done the construction was solid; better than new."

"So, the wagon wasn't covered, then?"

"No, but Zach could always add a frame and some canvas. But they left with so little: some clothes, two bedrolls and a few personal items. Zach also bought fifty pair of Levi 501 work pants, thinking that they could sell them at a big profit in Bodie. That heavy denim with the three riveted pockets could last a miner a whole season of work. The entire load was covered with a canvas."

"You must be sorry to see Zach go."

"I am. I told him that I'll always have a job open for him whenever."

"Bill, what did you think of the two of them as mates? You know, she's a college graduate from a wealthy and sheltered background and he's a hardworking, get-your-hands-dirty guy who might have finished high school. "

"You ever see Megan?"

"No, but I have a photo her folks gave me. Looks like a pretty girl."

"She's just not some pretty girl, Clay. She is a beautiful woman in every way. Stands about five foot six, well built with the curves in all the right places, full lips, and she is poised and articulate, and…"

"Whoa, Bill. Don't get carried away. I get the picture. Maybe it's a good thing Zach took her away from here."

"You know what I mean, Clay. At my age I still enjoy seeing a beautiful woman, and she is the finest."

"Well, OK, that's what Zach might see in her, but what does she see in him?"

"Zach is a tall, strong and well-built young man and easily attracted to a young determined woman. He isn't as talkative, but what he says is always honest and straight from the heart. He has a calmness about him that I think makes her feel comfortable in his presence. He is not a take charge sort of guy, but he always respects her needs and her independence. He gives, but he doesn't take. On the other hand, I often felt that he was holding back his emotions, like he was afraid to let people know how he really felt."

"Bill, you're making this sound all too ideal, but I respect your opinion. You haven't been wrong yet. Of course, there is always a first time, and he does sound a little weak-kneed to me." And with that Bill gave Clay a poke on the arm, and they laughed with mutual understanding of each other developed over those many years.

"So, what's your plan, Clay?"

"Well, they have almost a week's head start. They left on Wednesday and Williams did not come to hire me until Monday, and I didn't get here to see him and take the assignment until this morning. It's too late to do anything more today. I plan on taking the ferry from Martinez to Sacramento tomorrow. They probably take the route through Placerville and over Echo Summit to Lake Tahoe and then to Carson City and then head south about one hundred and twenty miles to Bodie. I'd say it will take them all of two weeks if those two horses hold up well. I'll take the same route, but I know of a short cut heading south just before one reaches Lake Tahoe.

That will take me about eight days to reach Bodie by horseback."

"Anything I can do to help, Clay?"

"Yes, there is. Those two ranch hands of Williams have been following me everywhere I've gone. Probably hoping to follow me on my search. I have a plan. I'm going to ride out of here in a few minutes and head south for about ten miles. There is a cemetery I know of and I'm going to walk among the grave sites for a few minutes and pause for a long and quiet moment in front of one of the graves. Any one will do. Then I'll ride back and spend the night here\, in your tack room, if that's okay. While I'm gone, have one of your men go to the steamer depot in Martinez and reserve a space for me and my horse on the 2:30 ferry bound for Sacramento. When it's time for me to go tomorrow, we'll work out another diversion to elude Williams's men."

"You got it Clay, and here, take this bouquet of flowers that my secretary left on the counter this morning. You can place it beside the grave. Also, use my black gelding now and I'll have my man use the same horse later when he rides out to lure them away from you. Do it up real good."

Within a few minutes, Jameson saddled Heck's gelding and rode the ten miles south and stopped and the Methodist cemetery, walked along the grave sites and finally settling on one, a Harriet C. Walker, *1813 -1869, May She Rest in Peace.* He knelt beside the headstone and gently placed the flowers at its base. He absorbed himself in deep thought for a long moment, and then rose, walked to his horse, mounted, and rode back to Bill Heck's place. He observed Rand and Scully following him the entire trip. They weren't too bright, he decided.

Riding Heck's black gelding was a nice touch. Before he would leave for the ferry, he would have Heck, or someone, dress like him and ride the gelding back to the cemetery for some additional repose.

Chapter 4

Megan busied herself sorting out the few clothes and personal items she would pack for her trip with Zach. A honeymoon, and a new adventure in life with the man she loved. It felt so much like a dream, and a dream that she could not share with her parents because Zach and Megan were going to elope and leave without telling them.

Megan had mixed feelings. She loved her mother very much and knew that her mother would be hurt by not being a part of her only daughter's wedding. But that's the price they would both have to pay to avoid the reactions from her father. And she had to get away from here.

Her father had always been a dominate force in her life and had endeavored to mold her into the woman he wanted her to be. She knew that he doted on her, as well, but when she spoke of plans to marry Zach Barnes, all hell broke loose. Her father went into a tirade that lasted three days. He fired Zach, who had been working on the ranch for a few months, and he warned Zach to never set foot on his property and never have contact with his daughter if he valued his life. He treated both his ranch and his daughter as his property.

When Zach and Megan first spoke of marriage, she wanted to elope the next day. Zach's calmer and more realistic view of their situation prevailed. Megan had one more semester at college to finish her degree and obtain a teaching certificate, which might come in handy at some point in their lives. He had time to complete the re-building of three wagons for Mr. Finley, a customer of Consolidated Freight, where Zach had found new and good employment.

As she finished packing and reflected on the past few months, she felt tremendous relief at having graduated. The pressure of study was over and she had fulfilled that expectation which her parents had laid on her. However, she realized now that it had been worth the effort. Her experiences at Mills College in Oakland had not only given her the degree and teaching credential that prepared her for a job, it shaped her view of the world and gave her an appreciation of life and people.

Megan had hoped to take over running her father's business interests, gradually, as he slacked off, but she knew now that he wanted a man to run the business. He was bitter about his sons leaving.

Megan was a beautiful woman in every way. She blended a natural sensuality with poise and confidence, and an easy-going manner, as to be admired by both men and women; usually for different reasons, of course.

She was aware of her own beauty and charm, but she also knew that there were many other women equally as beautiful, and she treated everyone as an equal. No more and no less, one from another. She was outgoing and friendly toward everyone she met without letting her ego get in the way. *How* she looked was not what mattered to her. Who she was and what she did with her life was important.

She had a commanding presence; she knew what gave meaning to her life; and she intended to control every aspect of her life to fulfill her destiny, as she called it. And she wasn't going to let her father get in the way. It was her life, not his. And a life as Mrs. Zach Barnes was now what she wanted. Zach gave her the strength and security she wanted, and the love and respect she needed. She was his equal, not his property. It also was a chance to get away.

Megan finished packing and dressed for bed. She didn't feel sleepy, however. Her mind was already taking the trip and she was imagining all sorts of wonderful scenarios of their new adventure in life together. Finally, in the middle of one of the scenarios she drifted into a deep sleep.

Zach pack what few personal belongings he possessed, along with supplies for their trip and those to sell in the Bodie store. He was anxious to leave, yet it was with mixed emotions.

This idea of marrying and eloping, and then going to Bodie just seemed to snowball from a comment by Megan to today, and to the forthcoming wedding. How did this all evolve? Was this his idea of hers? And did he really want to quit his job? It had been a good job.

Zach remembered his Uncle Harry as a carefree spirit, without much of a sense of responsibility. He seemed to be living the good life in Bodie, according to his letters, and he looked forward to Zach joining him. Zach didn't give it much more thought.

Zach and Megan were married at 10:00 o'clock on that Wednesday, June 23, 1893, in the parlor of his parents' home, with Reverend James Raney performing the ceremony. There were no actual bride's maids or best man. Only Zach's parents, and Bill Heck, Zach's employer and friend. But Megan was so thrilled that she was about ready to explode with joy.

Megan and Zach knew of each other while they were growing up in Andersville, but they had never given each other a second look until Zach came to work for Williams. Once he was working at the ranch, however, their lives seem to cross often. Zach made it happen as often as he could. Megan soon realized that Zach was the man for her and her life had taken a quick turn into emotional ecstasy and love. He also was her way out of town. This moment of their wedding was the fulfillment of their plans and the knowledge that her dreams of love were now a reality.

After the tearful goodbyes and hugs all around, they left in their wagon. From the rear of the wagon, Megan had hung a small hand-made sign, *Bound for Bodie*.

They arrived at the Martinez Ferry Depot just before 2:00 p.m. A ferry was waiting, with its engine running.

The ferry was named *Onward*. It was a single smoke stack sternwheeler, about 165 feet in length; one of many that plied the Sacramento River from the San Francisco and Oakland bay areas. It had been built in 1877 and the white paint still had a gleam to it. However, by steamboat standards it was medium sized, compared to many of the other river boats, such as the luxurious 245-foot paddlewheel steamer, *Chrysopolis* that had been sailing from the bay area up the Sacramento River for years.

The *Onward* had a good safety record, which meant that it had never suffered a boiler explosion as had several of the other steamers.

The Captain of the *Onward* was a Danish man, Edward Hansen. He welcomed Zach and Megan aboard and led them to the large sleeping cabin they had reserved on the second deck. Thereafter, Zach led the horses from the dock to the lower deck of the steamer, and unhitched the horse and put them in two of the several stalls intended for their travel.

The *Onward* got underway at exactly 2:30 p.m. The sky was clear and the temperature was in the mid-80s, and there was a gentle southerly breeze blowing off the water. The couple spent most of the afternoon and early evening sitting out on the forward deck enjoying the river and the sights along the way. They dined there as well. Megan noted how the river was often lined with beautiful trees, and here and there, they were draped with festoons of wild grape vines. There were many farms on both sides of the river along the way and many reflected the wealth of the farmers, with beautiful homes, rich soil and fine orchards.

In the evening the beams of the nearly full moon danced along the water and created such a peaceful scene, and romantic scene.

Without saying a word, Megan took Zach's hand and led him back to their cabin. The room was dimly lit by a small lantern. They faced each other, holding hands, for an awkward moment. Zach was not sure what to do next.

Megan had had experiences like this in her mind many times over, and she knew what she wanted to do. She.put her arms around Zach and kissed him tenderly and said, "Mr. Barnes, we are now a couple ready to share with each other all we find in life. We shall share ourselves with each other unashamed and completely."

With that, Megan slowly unbuttoned Zach's shirt and peeled it back off of his shoulders. Then she removed all of her own clothes and stood naked before him. Then Zach quickly undressed. They embraced just standing there, and then they moved to the bed and began that wonderful first love of kissing, touching, and fondling, ending in the spasms of nature's rhythmic bliss.

It wasn't long, however, before they realized that they were not about to get any sleep or peace on the trip.

The ferry carried freight and stopped at every town to deliver or pick up items: Collinsville, Rio Vista, Isleton, Walnut Grove, and Courtland. It also stopped at many of the farms along the way. The constant jingle of the bell to the engine room about what speed to take, and the *toot* of the boat's whistle at every stop, were more than anyone could adjust to in just one night. However, they didn't let that interfere with their lovemaking.

The ferry landed at Eagle Point below Sacramento at 3:45 a.m. They unloaded their wagon and headed for Sacramento.

They arrived in downtown Sacramento at about 8:00 a.m. and went directly to Haymarket Square between 15th and 16th streets and "P' and "I" streets, where they found a place to wash and eat breakfast. It was a grand marketplace, with vendors showing a vast array of produce and crafted articles to buy. Zach watched their wagon while Megan wandered around the market stalls. She bought a variety of fruits and some biscuits to eat along the trip.

Chapter 5

Megan and Zach left Sacramento about 8:30 a.m. and headed toward the Sierras. They traveled about fifteen miles to Hangtown Crossing, rising in elevation from thirty feet above sea level to just over eighteen hundred feet, and then another three miles to a farm Megan had known about, owned by the Jenkins family. There was a sign on a fence post saying "meals provided." Mrs. Jenkins charged them $1.00 for fresh milk, cold chicken, and huckleberry pie. The air was warm and filled with the scents of the various pine trees in the area.

They left the Jenkins farm and headed up the road for Deer Creek. The road was very rough and the vegetation sparse. Most of it was hog-wallow, good for nothing but jack rabbits, grass hoppers, and wild turkeys Zach remarked. The air was still and hot.

They passed five small mining towns where it looked as though the mines had played out: Clarksville, Shingle Springs, White Rock Springs, Eldorado, and Diamond Springs. The towns were nearly deserted and the buildings were in disrepair, although Shingle Springs seemed to have more activity because it had some sort of rail center.

They reached Deer Creek fourteen miles later at about 5:00 p.m., where they rested the horses.

Deer Creek was a fine stream of clear cold mountain water flowing through groves of alder, sycamore, oaks and one large odd-looking tree that no one could identify, and just now it was covered with wine-colored pods similar in formation to those of the locust tree. It was a beautiful setting compared to the last fourteen miles.

"How much further do you want to travel today, Zach?"

"We still have plenty of day light left, Megan. Let's go on to the next town."

Megan was tired and sore from riding in the wagon for so long. She also felt grimy and wanted a bath, or at least a chance to wash her hands and face. She didn't say anything, however.

They reached Placerville about 8:00 p.m. It was a busy mining town with about 2,500 inhabitants. It was beautifully situated in a narrow valley among low hills.

The business streets ran through the narrow valley and extended out between the hills while most of the best residences were built on the hillsides, and the hills were covered with pines. There were two large box factoriesand a flour mill, which must have given work to a number of men. In fact, Megan wondered about seeing so many men wandering the streets and coming in and out of the bars.

Several of the men ran alongside the wagon trying to sweet-talk her, and one hung over the wagon's side as if trying to climb aboard. Megan looked at Zach, but he seemed oblivious to the scene. Finally, Megan chased the man away by hitting him with a parasol she had been carrying to protect her from the sun.

"Zach, why didn't you chase that man away? He was trying to get into our wagon."

"He was okay, Megan. He's just funning."

"Megan wasn't reassured, and she stared at Zach.

On the outskirts of town Megan saw a sign in front of a house with a barn offering camping in the nearby meadow. They drove in and the owner, a Mrs. Ross came out to greet them. She showed them where to set up camp. She also showed them her barn where they could stall the horses. The front stall was very large and filled with clean hay. Zach unhitched the horses, rubbed them down and gave them feed and water. They bought a sack of barley feed for $1.10 from Mrs. Ross. And she charged an additional $2.00 for camping and supper of venison stew and corn bread, with wild honey.

Outside the moon was a day past full, but was very bright, and they could see the entire yard, house, and surrounding area. The air was cool and calm, and the only noises they heard were sounds of the horses pulling at some hay.

"It's so peaceful here, Zach. I'm glad we came this far today."

They laid out their blankets on the fresh hay in the barn. They cuddled close, which led to their love-making. After that, sleep came quickly.

They left Placerville at about 6:15 a.m. following an improved version of the old Johnson Cut-off, going east from Placerville, over Peavine Ridge, and eventually returning to the trail along the American River and rising to over four thousand feet in elevation near Kyburz. They began another steep climb for about five hours until they reached Ten Mile House, where Megan fixed them lunch of bread, cheese, and fruit.

It must have been a tedious job to make this portion of the road from Placerville. It had required felling pine, then blasting the stumps and the many granite boulders all along the way. The road was still rough and they let the horses walked easy to spare their energy. The steepest climb up and then down was yet to come.

In the early evening they passed Pacific House and by 8:00 p.m. they crossed Moore's Bridge at Riverside. For the past two days they had crossed numerous small streams, and since leaving Placerville the road took them through forests of pine, cedar, spruce and fir. Now, two miles from Riverside, the road began paralleling the north fork of the American River, and it would continue that way until they reached the summit.

They had planned to stay the night at Riverside, at the suggestion of Mrs. Ross However, when they got there they found that thirteen cattlemen were already there, with a herd of 600 cattle that they were driving over the summit and on to Hope Valley for summer grazing. Six of the men were staying in the three bedrooms available at Riverside House and seven were sleeping in the barn.

Megan was flustered at first, but she approached one of the cowboys and said, "My husband and I have ridden a long way to day and I could sure use a good night's sleep. Any chance we could trade for your sleeping quarters in the house?"

The cowboy moved closer to her and asked, "What did you have in mind for a trade?"

Megan realized that he was flirting with her, and she blushed and backed a few steps away.

Zach was looking on, and was getting jealous and irritated. "Never mind, Megan. We'll be fine sleeping in the barn.'

The cowboy smiled and took on a polite tone, "No, I was just teasing the little lady. Of course, me and Jeb will take the barn and you can have the room. We've no hold on it."

"Thank you."

"We really appreciate it, Said Megan." And no more was said. The cost was $1.00 for the horses and $.50 for them to use a bedroom.

Riverside was a beautiful setting at night. Zach and Megan stood at their bedroom window and gazed at the night. The moon was still almost full and for a time shone down on the house and barn.

"Listen, Zach, you can hear the river dashing and tumbling over large rocks and into pools below. Such a peaceful sound."

"Sure, Megan," Zach replied, and he moved close to her and initiated their love-making.

By 7:00 a.m., Zach and Megan were dressed and down at the wagon hitching the horses and stowing their bedrolls as they prepared for another day's journey. To some, their journey might seem like an arduous trek, but to Megan and Zach it was an adventure, a beginning of their new life together.

They traveled about seven miles to the Johnson House, where they had breakfast of milk and biscuits with homemade jam. Zach got some coffee as well. It was a small summer resort on the banks of the river, with grand forested mountains and river scenery. It offered camping, good trout fishing, croquet grounds, hammocks, and a friendly host. Megan said she wanted to come back here someday to spend some time just enjoying the facilities and scenery.

While they were here, the cowboys they had met at Riverside passed by driving their cattle to grazing pastures.

From Johnson's they rode another twelve miles to Strawberry Valley House and camped in the large meadow. The cowboys were there as well with their cattle.

The road was still very rough and had been blasted out of rock. It often felt as though they were traveling over a wash board.

The horses were watered and fed and stalled in the barn for $1.00. Zach spread out their bedrolls on the ground near the barn in preparation for their night's sleep, while Megan built a small cooking fire within a circle of small rocks and placed a grate on it. Mrs. Johnson had given Megan two pieces of chicken to take with them on the trip. She cooked them on the grate, along with a pot of rice for dinner.

After dinner, they were invited to walk a short distance up the road to the Watson house, where they were welcomed by Mrs. Watson and her daughter, Tess. The Watsons had a violin and a piano, and Mrs. Watson began playing while Tess and Megan sang. It wasn't long before several of the cowboys walked up and joined the group and they all spent an enjoyable evening's entertainment.

Tess played a violin solo and then Megan sang one of her favorite Welsh songs taught to her as a young girl by her mother, *We'll keep a Welcome in the Hillside*. This prompted Joe, one of the cowboys to sing two cowboy ballads, while strumming on his guitar. He said that he often sang ballads to the herds at night to quiet the cattle. He and the other cowboys also flirted with Megan. She enjoyed the attention, but Zach just became sullen.

They left Strawberry Valley House about 9:00 a.m., but it was Sunday and Megan wanted to make it primarily a day of rest. Consequently, they drove only about seven miles to Phillips Station.

This was a dairy ranch during the summer months and because of the late summer it wouldn't be occupied until next week. They camped for the day and night.

Phillips was a meadow that Megan found more beautiful than Strawberry, and she took a sweeping view of the scenery, with her arms outstretched and said that since coming among the mountains she had a feeling of awe and reverence for what God had created.

Zach looked bored and walked to the stream behind the camping area and panned for gold, using a pie pan from their supply kit. He didn't find any.

Phillips was a beautiful meadow over 5,000 feet in altitude surrounded by mountains nearly another 1,500 feet high. One of the cowboys had told them of a lake at the top of the mountain directly across from Phillips meadow. It was called Cup Lake, he told them, and it was small round, with sides sloping in like a small tea cup. Megan all looked up to the top of the mountain and imagined what the lake would look like.

The mountain was studded with pine about half way up, and then covered with varying sizes of granite rocks. Summer had been late in coming and portions of the hillside were still blanketed with snow, depending upon their exposure to the day's sun. There was snow as well in the areas in full shade near the road. Megan said she would climb up to Cup Lake if she ever came this way later in the summer.

Megan spent the day reading and napping, while Zach tended the horses and checked the harnesses and the wagon as well as the brakes. They would need to depend on those brakes soon, when they made their way down the mountains.

Two of the cattlemen rode by, telling them that they hoped to move a third of the cattle on a trail around Echo Lake to a grassy area called Haystack Meadows and that they were on their way to the lake to see if the trail was passable. The lake was about three miles further up the road, near the summit, and about one mile north up a very rough road.

They returned in about two hours saying that the snow was ten feet deep in places around the lake and would not be passable for the cattle. Therefore, they would take all the cattle over the summit and down to Meyers and then over Luther Pass to Hope Valley for summer grazing.

That evening, Megan and Zach took their camp mattresses into the barn, where they settled in for the night.

During breakfast the next morning, they watched the cattlemen herd the cattle past them and up the grade toward the summit. It would be a long day for those men.

They left Phillips Station at about 9:00 a.m. Monday and headed for Echo Summit, a relatively steep climb of three miles. They were about an hour behind the cattle drive. They reached the summit in just over two hours. Zach stopped and dismounted from the wagon while he checked the wagon, harnesses, and brakes one more time.

The decent down from the summit to the valley floor at Meyers was four miles of steep and narrow road with three curves and sheer drop-offs on the outside of the road. Much of it had been chiseled and blasted out of granite boulders. Portions of the road at the top still had snow piled up along the inside which meant that the two left wheels would be riding through snow while the two outside wheels would be on hard granite.

Megan was anxious. She looked at Zach and asked, "Is it going to be alright going down?"

"It'll be fine, Megan. Not to worry." He seemed calm and very much at ease. That made her feel relaxed as well.

They could look over the edge and see a large canyon below that was forested with pine and groves of Aspen scattered along the American River.

They were half way down when a pile of small rocks spilled from the side of the cliff and scattered under the horses. They reared and started off at a fast pace. It appeared to Zach that one of the rein straps had snapped as well, and was trailing under the wagon. He rose immediately from the box and leaped onto the back of the inside horse, the left horse, the one who was the lead of the team. He grabbed hold of the broken rein, and then the other rein, and pulled back and down hard, talking to the horses in a calming voice as he did.

The horses responded well and quieted down. Zach remained on the back of the lead horse until they reached the bottom of the grade, where he quickly repaired the broken rein with a rawhide splice, upset with himself for not noticing the weakened harness earlier, when he checked them.

Megan tensed and was white-knuckled watching Zach. However, when the horsed calmed down she began to relax. She admired the way Zach had acted so quickly.

Once on the valley floor, Zach and Megan breathed a sigh of relief and they drove the team the short distance to Myers Station, another dairy ranch run by a family named Boswell, where they stopped for lunch. The Boswell girls had picked wild strawberries from the nearby field, and Mrs. Boswell brought Megan some homemade butter and a gallon of milk. She made a fine lunch of the strawberries and some leftover biscuits, with the butter.

The Boswell farm was at the crossroads where the main road continued on straight to Lake Tahoe, and then continued around the lake part way, then over Spooner Summit and down to Carson City. Bodie would be about 120 miles south then on a fairly level and good road.

The cowboys had turned south at the Boswell farm and drove their cattle over Luther Pass to Hope Valley for grazing. There was a shortcut from there toward Bodie, west along the south fork of the Carson River. A single rider on horseback, however, could save several days' time, but the road was too rough and rocky for wagon travel. Zach and Megan continued on toward Lake Tahoe.

They arrived at the Cascade House on the shore of Lake Tahoe, near the state line of Nevăda at about 4:00 p.m. They were met by a Mrs. Clemens, who managed the facilities that included a restaurant, sleeping cabins, and camp grounds with private beach area.

For the fee of $1.50, Zach and Megan were given a camping spot next to a grove of sugar pine trees only fifty yards from the lake. Their space had a large wooden table, with attached benches, and a cook stove. There were two communal outhouses, one at each end of the camping grounds. For an additional $.25, they arranged to take a hot bath inside the Cascade House. Megan tried to slip in the bathing room and share Zach's tum with him, but he was concerned that they might be caught and he said they had better not risk it.

After their baths, Megan cooked a light supper, and then spent the evening taking in the wondrous sights before them. They talked very little.

They sat near the lake to watch the magic of nature change the day into night. The beautiful lake before them, the tall sugar and pole pines behind them, and the snow-capped mountains were all about them.

As evening slowly crept in, Megan sat in awe of the gorgeous sunset. Zach dozed off and on. The Lake, always brilliant with color, became a mass of rainbow colors and the hills became great banks of misty purple, and they watched the sky as the brilliant red changed to orange, and then to gold, and then the orange, red, green and gold mingled and faded, and they were surrounded by the misty purple of twilight. Finally, Megan said, "Behind the sunset are the hills of God."

Megan got yeast and butter from Mrs. Clemens that evening and had put bread to rise over night. In the morning she baked it in the camp stove, and they had a fine breakfast of trout caught by Zach, fresh strawberries, and the fresh baked bread with newly churned butter.

It was the Fourth of July and there were many people on the beach and on the trails nearby. They decided to just laze about for another day enjoying the sun and beach. During the day they heard of some disconcerting events that had occurred near them. A cabin just down the beach from them had caught fire and burned early in the morning because of a defective flue. The fire also spread to a small grove of sugar pine next to the cabin and one passer-by said, "It caused a brilliant and awe-inspiring pyrotechnic display." Fortunately, the fire didn't spread further and was extinguished.

Later in the afternoon, four men had set sail from Glenbrook, a resort on the east side of the lake. They got drunk and were caught out on the lake when the afternoon breeze came up, making whitecaps on the water. Their boat tipped over and the four men drowned. Mrs. Clemens was heard to say, "We know not the time when the Lord shall come for us."

"Amen to that," echoed Megan.

During the afternoon, a group of five rowdy young men started to set up their camp between that of Megan and Zach, partially cutting off their view of the lake. Megan confronted them, saying that this was their camp site, but the men ignored her.

Zach didn't say a word, so Megan asked him, "Isn't there something you can do with them. They're deliberately cutting off our view of the lake."

"There's plenty of room for all of us, Megan. There is no need to make trouble over it."

Zach's response angered Megan. She wondered when a situation would reach a point when he felt that there was a need to make trouble. Or would Zach always let trouble slide, without dealing with it.

The next morning Zach loaded the wagon, hitched the horses, and they were off for Spooner Summit and Carson City, and then on to Bodie.

The trip took five long days. There was very little conversation and no love-making on the way.

Chapter 6

Jameson had been advised by Heck not to display any weapons on the ferry ride; they would just look out of place. Consequently, he packed his Colt 1873 Frontier model .44 caliber revolver and holster in the saddle bags that held his clothes, and put his Winchester '73 rifle in the saddle scabbard.

1873 was a good year for guns. Both the Colt and the Winchester were chambered in .44-40 caliber center fire cartridges, a vast improvement over the .44 caliber rim fire of the Henry rifle he previously used. The 1886 version of the Winchester was a better rifle, but that John Browning design was chambered in .45-70 caliber which wouldn't match that used in his revolver. Thus, Jameson had to compromise.

As he dressed for the trip, Jameson traded his business dress clothes for something more practical for the trip: a pair of Levi Strauss & Company blue indigo dyed cotton twill denim waist overalls, leather suspenders over a dark cotton shirt, a buckskin vest, a blue kerchief tied loosely around his neck, and his Stetson hat. He chose this style of Stetson because it made him look taller than he really was.

He remembered reading some years ago that this was the reason Sir Robert Peal had his Bobbies of the London police force wear the tall helmets. It can have an intimidating effect, especially if it is combined with an imposing manner.

He also packed an extra pair of waist-overalls, two shirts, and three pair of sox. 1873 had also been a good year for the style of waist overalls he wore because that was the year that the Levi Strauss & Company added the three riveted pockets to the sewn seams, and a rivet at the bottom of the button fly, and by 1886 it added the leather patch on the back of the pants with the logo, *The Two Horse® Brand.* However, a pair from Lot 501 cost about $1.50 each, which was about six hours pay for the average workman, but they were well worth the price; and Jameson earned much more than the average workman.

His working boots were well worn, but were comfortable, and had many years of service left in them. A sheath that held a Bowie knife had been sewn inside the right boot.

Jameson walked into the stable yard behind the store and found that his horse had already been saddled by Heck. She was a six-year-old blue dun mare, which Jameson had unceremoniously named *Blue*. Heck had included Clay's bedroll, and had placed some food stuffs and small coffee pot in the saddlebags. He was standing there holding the reins.

"Well, thanks, Heck. I was just coming to do that very thing."

"Thought I'd see you off, Clay. Here take this," and he handed Clay a scabbard with a gun inside.

"What is it?

"It's a Model 1893 Winchester 12-gauge pump shotgun. This one was sent to me to try out by a young gunsmith friend of mine, John Browning. I worked with him at his father's shop in Utah and we became friends. He's a young visionary when it comes to guns. He sold his design for this gun to the Winchester Repeating Arms Company and moved to Connecticut to help with the production and to design other guns for the company. John is always moving forward, designing guns faster than they can be produced, and this one he sent me is a prototype for the next version of the model. I already had one from the first production, but John said that this one is tougher and stronger. He strengthened the frame and closed it at the top so the fired cartridges are ejected out the side. It has a 20-inch barrel and holds five 2 5/8-inch cartridges. Point it at a crowd and watch them scatter in all directions."

"You think I'm going to need more fire-power, do you?"

"Well, you're heading into the Devil's playground and I figured that this might help get you out. And I tied a small sack of food and a few utensils to your saddle horn and hung a canteen of fresh water there too."

"Thanks, Heck. Want to come along and cook my dinners too?"

"You go on. It's almost 2:00 o'clock. Mustn't keep the ferry waiting. Get on with your business. I'll be waiting for you. Give me a few minutes now to get you ready. I had Jimmy, one of my clerks, dress up like you might be, and there he goes, riding my black gelding to the cemetery. It should decoy them just as we planned.

Just then one of Heck's other clerks poked his head out the back door to say that Jimmy had been followed by two men on horseback.

"Time to go, Clay," said Heck. And bring back my gun in one piece."

For Clay, each job was an adventure. *What strange happenings would this one bring*, he mused. And he rode down to the docks and boarded the ferry, the *Onward*.

Jameson bedded his horse in one of the several stalls on the lower deck. He laid his saddle, with its saddle bags and gun scabbards, near the front of the stall, making it inconvenient for anyone to reach for them without disturbing the horse, and then he went to the upper deck t watch the scenery drift by. The *Onward* left the dock at exactly 2:30pm.

The day was warm and the air clear. There was a gentle southerly breeze blowing off the water. Jameson soon realized that this was going to be a slow trip because the ferry stopped at all the towns and many of the farms along the way, delivering goods, and loading on goods to deliver back to the bay area.

After eating a light supper offered by the ship's steward, Jameson retired to the stall area below for what he hoped would be a restful sleep. However, he was disturbed every so often by the toot of the ferry's whistle.

The ferry stopped at Eagle Point, below Sacramento at about 4:00 am, and Jameson saddled *Blue* and rode to Sacramento. He arrived at Haymarket Square at about 6:00 am, and found it thriving with both wholesalers and local farmers and merchants selling their foods and wares retail out of make-shift stalls. He enjoyed a mug of coffee and a biscuit, and then headed toward Placerville, also known as Hangtown because so many claim jumpers had been hanged there over the years.

He passed several played-out mining towns along the way and stopped at one called Shingle Spring when he read a sign on a building "Food Served." He had a plate of venison stew and a cold coffee, then rode on to Placerville, where he stopped at the local livery stable. He had the man there rub down *Blue* and feed her. That cost him a dollar, along with another dollar for the privilege of sleeping in a hay pile near his horse.

Jameson smoothed out a place in the hay, spread out his soogan, and placed his saddle at the head for a pillow. He decided that from this point on he would travel armed, so he strapped on his gun belt and made sure his Colt was loaded and his belt was filled with cartridges. Then he walked up the street looking for a quiet saloon.

He quickly discovered that there were many saloons, but none of them were quiet. It was a rowdy town, he thought. He finally entered *Dink's Palace*, a saloon where the clientele seemed more absorbed in playing poker than drinking and yelling. He walked up to the bar and ordered a beer and a shot of rye, which he quickly poured into the glass of beer. He took a large swig and let out a long aaaaaah.

The bartender watched Jameson take his drink and walked up to face him, ready to engage his customer in conversation. He was a man who loved to talk, no matter who would listen.

"My name's Dink, friend. Welcome to *Dink's Palace*, the pleasure dome of Hangtown. Who do I have the pleasure of serving?" He was short and round in the middle and balding on the top, and had a whiskey red complexion. He beamed a smile from ear to ear.

"My pleasure, Dink. People call me Clay."

"That's quite a drink you made, pouring the rye into the beer. I never seen anyone do that before."

"I like it," replied Jameson. "It's known as Montana spring water."

"You from Montana?"

"I've been there."

"You a stranger in town, aren't you?"

"Isn't every one!" Jameson offered as a statement, not a question.

"Where're you from," queried the bartender.

"Just about everywhere." Jameson took another long drink of his beer, emptied the glass and motioned for another.

"You want another rye, too," asked the bartender.

"They go together, don't they," replied Jameson.

The bartender poured the beer and rye and placed them before Jameson, who proceeded to pour the rye into the beer and take a drink.

"Looking for someone?" asked Dink.

"Why would you ask that," said Jameson.

"I seen you give the whole place a quick scan when you first came in, and you're standing there at the curved end of the bar from where you can watch most everyone here. Also, you come in with a sidearm strapped on. Not many folks hereabouts wear a sidearm."

"You're very observant, Dink. You must be a student of human behavior."

"I ain't no student, Clay, but I've learned a lot about people from running this place over the years."

"I'll bet you have, Dink. I'll bet you have." Jameson didn't offer any response to Dink's question or to his characterization of him.

"You're not much of a talker," quipped Dink.

"No, Dink, I'm not much of a talker, unless I have something to say. I'm not much of a listener either."

Jameson downed the rest of his Montana spring water and placed the glass on the bar. "Thanks for the drinks," and he turned and walked toward the door, leaving Dink standing there with his mouth half open ready to say something.

On the way out, a large scruffy looking man with a thick and unruly head of black hair and a beard to match raised his arm in front of Jameson, as if to bar the doorway. "Hey stranger, sit down and have a drink with Manny, here. Manny needs someone to talk to."

"No thanks. Two is my limit," and Jameson pushed slightly against the man's arm.

"I asked you nicely, friend. Sit down and have a drink," and the man started to rise from his chair.

Jameson quickly gripped the fleshy portion of the top of Manny's shoulder just above the clavicle and squeezed hard. He had a grip like a vise. The man's arm dropped limply at his side and he winced in pain.

"No need for you to get up, Manny. I'll see myself to the door." And he gave the man an extra squeeze and pushed himself off toward the door.

Manny sat there in obvious pain, but looked down and tried to hide it. He made no more gesture toward Jameson.

Jameson walked up the boardwalk and turned at the nearest ally and walked up behind the other buildings and entered the stable by the rear door, just in case Manny or someone had tried to follow him. He was accustomed to avoiding trouble unless it was of his concern, and then he responded directly and completely.

He didn't consider himself aggressive, only assertive, and there was a difference in his mind. He didn't mind other people's business, but neither did he allow others mind his business.

He lay on top of his soogan for several minutes, listening for both the usual and unusual sounds, and after being satisfied that all was well, he fell asleep.

Chapter 7

The man at the livery stable was called Fuzz. In the morning, he handed Jameson a mug of coffee and offered to saddle Jameson's horse.

"Sure Fuzz. I appreciate it." He handed Fuzz a silver dollar for his efforts, mounted, and rode out the door and headed east.

It was just after 6:00 a.m. when Jameson left Placerville. He followed the old Johnson cut-off, over Peavine Ridge, and eventually returned to a trail that paralleled the American River. The elevation had been rising slowly but steadily and it began a steep rise from here to Kyburz, where it reached nearly 4,000 feet. It would rise at an even steeper climb from this point to the summit.

Jameson allowed *Blue* to walk at an easy pace, and he stopped twice along the way to rest and water the horse as well as himself. He lunched on hardtack that Heck had stowed in the food sack, tied to his saddle horn. Heck had made his hardtack by adding honey to the flour and water, which gave it a subtle, sweet taste.

Jameson reached Riverside House by 6:00 pm and decided to enjoy a room with a bed instead of roughing it on the ground near the river. For $.50 he fed his horse and bedded him in the barn, then spent another $.50 for his own bed and $1.00 for Mulligan Stew and black coffee, blended with chicory and topped with thick rich fresh cream. The aroma and taste of it reminded Jameson of New Orleans, where he had frequently enjoyed that blended as well straight roasted chicory.

Jameson was up by 5:00 a.m., and after two mugs of the delicious coffee-chicory blend and a large piece of cornbread, he was back on the trail.

He reached Strawberry Valley House about three hours and twenty miles later. There, he lunched on hardtack and fresh stream water and rested his horse for about thirty minutes. From there, he rode another seven miles to Phillips Station, and then another three miles to Echo Summit.

During these last few miles, Jameson felt as though he was at the top of the world. He had reached 5,000 feet and was surrounded by the Sierra Nevada Mountains, another 1,500 feet high, along with forests of pine. The streams and river along the way were graced with alder and popular trees, whose leaves fluttered in the gentle breeze.

At the summit, the elevation was approximately 7,400 feet. Jameson looked out and saw the deep blue color of Lake Tahoe, a lake of infinite beauty, surrounded by more forested land. It had to be the eighth wonder of the world, he mused. Summer was late in coming this year because he could see that many of the mountains were still flanked with snow.

The decent from the summit was three miles long and about 1,000 feet down. It was steep and slippery in places where the snow was still on the road, but had turned to ice when melting. Jameson walked *Blue* down the curvy road bed, keeping close to the bank side so as not to get close to the steep cliff on the outside. It took them almost an hour to descend.

Jameson re-mounted when they neared the bottom and rode the short distance along the valley floor to Myers Station Ranch, a dairy and inn run by the Boswell family. The station house first opened in 1851 as a hostelry and stage coach stop and trading post. It was also used as a pony express station for a short time. It was well known to travelers and was the hub for those heading in various directions. It had been owned and operated by the Boswell family now for about ten years.

Jameson checked in as an overnight guest and was shown a room where he could wash, and then shown to his bedroom where he would sleep for the night. Dinner, he was told would be served in the dining room in thirty minutes.

Mr. Boswell took Jameson's horse to the barn and rubbed him down and fed him on sweet oats. Mrs. Boswell fed Jameson and three other travelers on roasted chicken, with mashed potatoes and homemade butter, and a pie made with freshly picked strawberries. Her daughters helped set and clear the table. After dinner, Jameson cornered Mr. and Mrs. Boswell alone to ask what they might know about Zach and Megan Barnes.

"Mrs. Boswell, thanks so much for that great supper, and Mr. Boswell, I appreciate the way you cared for my horse. It's been a long trip and both my horse and I are thankful for your care. I'll be turning in for the night in a few minutes, but I wanted to ask you about some friends of mine. They are a young married couple traveling by wagon. I thought they might have stopped here."

Mr. and Mrs. Boswell glanced at each other and hesitated to answer. They were suspicious of Jameson's interest in the young couple. Finally, Mrs. Boswell spoke up.

"Sorry, Mr. Jameson. They don't sound familiar. Probably either didn't come this way or stopped somewhere else."

Neither one would look Jameson in the eye while she was talking, but they gave each other a quick glance. Jameson sensed that they had been warned to look out for strangers asking about them. He decided to be completely open and confide in them. It sensed that it was the only way he would get their cooperation.

He addressed them both: "Folks, let me explain the truth of what's going on here." He handed them one of his business cards. "You see, I am a private investigator, hired to find the couple."

He handed them photos of Zach and Megan. "This young couple, Zach Barnes and Megan Williams, recently married in his parents' home, without her parents' knowledge, and they have run away, as it were. Her father, Morgan Williams, is a cantankerous and demanding man who was totally against the two ever getting married and demands that his daughter live her life on his terms. He hired me to find her and bring her home, and if possible, to see that Zach never makes it home, or anywhere, for that matter. I told him that I would find them, but I would not force anything on either of them. If Megan wants to come home, I would escort her, and I certainly would not stop Zach from doing anything. I am here at the blessings of the parents of both Megan and Zach. I know and they know that Mr. Williams has sent two of his ranch hands to follow me and to bring her home, like it or not, and to kill Zach. I need to find Megan before they do."

Mrs. Boswell covered her open mouth with her hand and appeared startled at what I said about the two men planning to kill Zach.

"I am asking for your help is saving these two. I know they are heading for Bodie and that they came this way. All I want from you is to confirm that they did come this way and how long ago. I don't know for certain that the two men, Scully and Rand are their names, know where I have gone or that they will ever find me. My guess is that they will. I ask you to not share any information with anyone who might stop here asking about the couple."

There was a long silence and the Boswells looked at each other and she gave a nod to him.

Mr. Boswell said, "You are correct, Mr. Jameson. They did stop here for lunch and then moved on to stay at Lake Tahoe for a day or two before they left for Bodie. That was a week ago, on July 3rd. They seemed so happy and in love, and spoke of a new life together in Bodie. Zach seemed particularly anxious to reach his uncle and begin their business venture. I don't know much about Bodie, but I hear it is a rough place to live."

"It's worse than you can imagine, Mr. Boswell, and I will do everything I can to either help them get settled or, better yet, to move to a more agreeable place."

"And we'll do whatever we can to offer any information about them, or about you as well.

"Thanks, but don't put yourself in any danger."

"Over what?" offered Mrs. Boswell, and Jameson smiled and they exchanged knowing looks.

Jameson took the upstairs bedroom at the end of the hall. The sheets smelled freshly washed and the down comforter was soft and provided the warmth he needed during the cold night. He rose at 6:00 a.m., dressed and descended the stairs to the smell of freshly brewed coffee and hot cinnamon rolls.

"Mrs. Boswell, you know just how to treat a weary traveler. I thank you so much for your hospitality." She beamed at receiving the compliment.

After breakfast, Jameson went to the barn where he found that Mr. Boswell had his horse saddled and ready to go. He pointed at the rifle and the 12-gauge shotgun attached to the saddle and commented: "You must be expecting to confront an army."

"One can't be too careful, Mr. Boswell. I prepare for the worst and hope for the best and face whatever comes."

"Sounds like good advice. You take care, son."

"Thanks, I don't know any other way."

Chapter 8

Jameson rode south for about eighteen miles, taking the road over Luther Pass. The road rose gently for about fourteen miles to 7,700 feet at the summit. Then it was an even gentler ascent into the Carson River Canyon and Hope Valley, and ended at Woodfords, a settlement that at one time had served as a pony express remount station. There, it met an east-west road that paralleled the north fork of the Carson River for eighteen miles to Gardnerville, Nevăda.

Jameson saw what seemed like hundreds of cattle grazing all over the lush pasture land of Hope Valley. He saw several cowboys tending the herd as well. Mr. Boswell had mentioned the drive of cattle coming through Myers Valley on the way to Hope Valley for summer grazing.

Jameson spoke to one of the cowboys who recalled passing Zach and Megan on their way to Echo Summit in a wagon, but didn't recall seeing them thereafter.

Blue had begun to pant and seemed labored coming through Luther Pass so Jameson decided to lay over her for the night to rest her and then get an early start in the morning for Gardnerville. The Menzies family ran a small inn at Woodfords and for $1.50 they gave him a supper of fresh trout and cornbread washed down with strong black coffee, and a cabin to use for the night.   They also provided a bucket of oats for *Blue* and all the hay she could eat.

The road to Gardnerville was narrow and rutty and would have been too rough on a wagon. Jameson followed it as it paralleled the Carson River for about twelve miles before the country opened up into a vast grassland, with Gardnerville off in the distance.   Three miles south of Gardnerville, Jameson found a place to camp for the night among a grove of cottonwood trees and next to a stream. He unsaddled *Blue*, rubbed her down, and tethered her at one end of the grove of trees next to the water, and where there was an abundance of grass for her to eat.

Whenever he woke during the night, he let the murmur of the cottonwood trees lull him back to sleep.

They got an early start the next morning and found the road easy traveling. Jameson took *Blue* at a slow gallop, alternating that with a walk for about a mile at a time. They rested twice along the way and arrived at Coleville at about 7:00 pm. This was a small settlement located in the Antelope Valley on the West Walker River. It had a post office, a store with a livery stable, and two saloons, one of which also served meals and had four rooms to rent.

Jameson left *Blue* and his saddle at the livery, but took his belongings up to a room above the saloon.

Back down at the bar, three men were playing poke at a table and two were standing at the bar having a drink. The bartender was a tall and slender middle-aged man with a neatly trimmed beard and long black hair, tied in a pony-tail.

"What can I get you," he asked.

Jameson ordered steak and eggs and a beer with a shot of rye as a chaser, only he didn't chase with it; he poured it right into the beer.

"Staying over long?" asked the bartender.

"Just passing through." Jameson replied.

"Where you headed?"

"South."

A cook brought out a plate of steak and eggs and placed it on one of the empty tables. It smelled good and asted better. Jameson was hungry. He washed down the food with another beer and shot of rye, and then walked outside and sat in an old wicker chair on the porch.

The sun was setting and the sky lit up the clouds that Jameson had not noticed before with colors that changed from yellow to red to purple. A beautiful transformation in nature. The temperature was dropping as quickly as the sun.

Jameson went to the livery and checked on *Blue*, and then went to his room for the night.

Up early in the morning. Coffee and a stale biscuit, and they were off south once more. The road followed the west fork of the Walker River, and the river was full and running fast. The noise of it dashing over the many rocks in the river bed covered any other sounds of the morning. If they kept up the good pace, they would make the twenty-six miles to Bridgeport by late afternoon.

Jameson arrived at about 7:00 p.m., tired and hungry.

The town was located in the middle of a large fertile valley where the locals farmed and grew a variety of fruits and vegetables which were traded on Saturday in the town square. The town was close to the border between

California and Nevăda and was the seat of Mono County. It boasted a large two story a court house built in 1880 in what they called the Italianate-style. It was the pride of the town.

Jameson left *Blue* at the livery stable, where an old whiskered man named Gus promised to rub her down and feed her well. He also promised to guard the saddle and Jameson's guns and bedroll. Jameson took his saddle bags into the better of the two hotels and was given a large room overlooking the street for $2.00. For an additional $1.00 he was offered a hot water bath and was guaranteed it would be first water.

After soaking in the tub for twenty minutes, Jameson dried, put on some clean underclothes, dressed, and went to the local barber shop for a shave. He felt as good as new. He then went to a nearby saloon for his usual beer and a shot of rye.

He stood at the end of the bar facing the door where he could see who came and went, and he could see most of the bar room as well. However, he didn't see a man, who must have entered by the back door, approach him from the left. By the time he was aware of the man, he was standing alongside and was smiling at him.

"Evening, stranger," said the man. He was a big man, husky, but not fat, with wide shoulders, a square jaw, and large penetrating eyes that seemed to look right through a person and know their soul. His dark red hair and neatly trimmed mustache were showing streaks of grey, revealing the aging of the man.

"Good evening to you. Is there something I can do for you?" Jameson's tone was sullen and demanding until he noticed the star on the man's vest lapel. "Oh, you're the sheriff. Is this a social call or business?"

"Well, you tell me."

"I'm not sure what you mean. My name's Jameson, sheriff. I'm stopping in your fair town for the night, on my way south. Just having a drink before turning in. Is there a problem?"

"Well, Mr. Jameson, here's the thing. A lot of strangers pass through my town, coming or going, living their own lives and not bothering anyone. I see them all and most don't give me any cause to be suspicious. But some do. I'm just checking more closely just to determine which way you fall.

"Well sheriff. Just like I said. I'm here for the night and then on my way. Now why would I make you suspicious?"

"Take a look around the room and tell me what you see."

Jameson scanned the room and noticed that three more men had entered the saloon since he had, making a total of eight. All behaving and minding their own business.

"I see a nice peaceful scene with eight men either playing poker or drinking. No problems here."

"Notice anything those men have in common that's different from you."

"You got me there, sheriff. I'm a little dense, I guess, but I don't get what you mean. What am I supposed to notice?"

"None of those men are armed, and you are. In fact, you are the only man I've seen today wearing a gun. And I've been informed that you have a 12-gauge shotgun and a Winchester rifle in their scabbards on your saddle, down at the livery. All that seems out of sorts to me, so I thought I'd inquire as to who you are and what need you have for all that firepower."

"Does this town have rules about being armed?"

"No. No rules. You just stand out enough to make me wonder why the need for the guns."

"I need the guns for my allergies, sheriff."

"Just what are you allergic to?"

"Snakes, sheriff. I'm concerned that I might run into snakes."

As Jameson was talking, it occurred to him that the sheriff might come in handy. He seems to watch everyone coming through town and he might be able to verify if and when Zach and Megan were here. He might also notice if and when Scully and Rand come this way and warn him.

"Now you're really peaking my curiosity. What kind of snakes are you concerned about?"

"Well, sheriff, if you have the time, I'll tell you the whole story."

"My time is yours."

Jameson reached into his vest pocket and took out one of his business cards and handed it to the sheriff. "As I said, my name is Clay Jameson. I work as a private investigator."

"Jameson, Clay Jameson. I think I've heard that name before. You ever worked for the Pinkerton agency?"

"Yes, I did. For five years."

"So, you're that Clay Jameson. Now it's coming together."

"Is that coming together a good one or a bad one?"

"That's a good one, so far. I was working as a deputy U. S. Marshal out of Abilene, Kansas during the '80s, when you Pinkerton men were chasing outlaws all over the country. Your name was mentioned often. One of the good guys. However, I need you to know that this is my town and I don't want any trouble here. It's a peaceful town, and I keep it that way."

"No need to worry, Sheriff. I really am just passing through. "I have been hired to find a young couple that ran off and left their parents worried, especially the girl's parents. If I find them and she will return home, I am to escort her. If not, I will help them get settled in whatever way I can."

"Sounds plain enough. What do they look like and where were they going?"

Jameson showed the sheriff the photos of Zach and Megan. "They would have come through here on a wagon within the past week, and they are heading for Bodie"

"Yes, I recall them two. He's a big strapping kid and she's a real beauty, wearing clothes that showed the best of her. Came through here only two days ago. If I knew they were going to Bodie, I'd a stopped them until I could talk some sense into them. Bodie is a hell hole, and those two will never survive, especially that young man. You should be able to find them easy enough, but the rest might be difficult, if they have a mind to stay."

"There's a little more to it, sheriff. The girl's father wants her back, but doesn't want her husband to return. He offered me $500 to end Zach's life right there. When I refused and said I would find them, but I would help her, he agreed to hire me, but he also sent two of his own ranch hands to follow me and bring her back, without Zach. They would probably want to take me out as well, since I would be in their way."

"Now I understand why all the firepower. Bodie is within my jurisdiction, but I don't go there unless I absolutely have to, and I never have to. I just figure that those folks will kill each other off, given enough time, and they don't need my help to do it. But if two snakes, to use your term, are coming through and are up to no good, I might be able to help."

"I was hoping you would make the offer. I can get into Bodie and get them out without much difficulty. However, I don't want to be waylaid on our way back."

"I'll keep an eye peeled, and if those two come through town, I'll arrest them on some charge and hold them until you get back. We can work out what to do next at that time."

"You can do that, sheriff?"

"Hey, like I said, it's my town and I aim to keep the peace. And I'll warn you, Clay, there is a guy in Bodie named Jake Tibbs. He is bad news. Don't cross him or irritate him unless you are sure you're faster than him. And if you see don't turn you back on him."

"Thanks, I'll remember that Sheriff. I like to keep things peaceful myself, but I don't mind shooting snakes is they rattle."

They shook hands and Jameson bought the drinks. After some friendly conversation they parted and Jameson went back to the hotel and to bed.

Chapter 9

Jameson was up by 6:00 a.m., had coffee and three eggs, with home-made sourdough bread and honey, and left the livery, heading for Bodie, within the hour.

Bodie was about twenty-four miles, with the last six miles over rough road. The road to Bodie forked left after about twelve miles. Thereafter, the bumps and ruts were more frequent. And for the first time, Jameson passed three sets of travelers along the way coming out of Bodie. Each time they warned Jameson not to descend into Hell.

Jameson arrived in Bodie at about 7:00 pm. The houses and small businesses were spread across the flat land of the valley and the mines were located at the top of a far hill. There was one long main street, with six or seven short, and one or two block cross streets. Main

Street looked the same as he remembered it: strewn with saloons, brothels and cheap hotels. He found a store with a large sign overhead reading *Barnes General Store and Warehouse* around the corner on Green Street. Behind the store, but with its entrance on Main Street, was McGuire's Livery Stable. There also was a sign hanging in the front window offering rooms to let.

Jameson entered the front of the livery, where he was greeted by the owners, Patrick and Molly McGuire, both of whom looked as rough and tough as they come; and the main difference between them was Patrick's full beard.

"What'll it be young man?" asked Molly.

"Bed and board for me and my horse, if it's available for both."

"Sure enough. $5.00 for you and $5.00 for your horse for the night."

"That's a little pricy, isn't it?"

"You can always go elsewhere, if you can find a room.   We only got three rooms, two upstairs and one down. You can take your pick."

"Down stairs will be just fine."

"Too late for supper, but I have some soup hot on the stove and I can give you some biscuits to sop it up with."

"That will do nicely."

"How long you planning to stay?"

"That all depends. I'll know more tomorrow. Here, I'll pay in advance for two nights." He handed Molly twenty dollars.

Patrick took Jameson's horse around to the back where the livery stables were, where he rubbed down the horse and gave it feed, while Molly led Jameson through a side door into a small dining area.

"There's a pan of water over there, if you've a mind to wash."

Jameson washed his hands, face and neck, then dried them with a clean towel on the rack above the pan. Everything looked old, but it was clean and neat. Not what he had expected.

Molly brought Jameson a large bowl of thick soup, the exact nature of which remained a mystery. Nevertheless, it was hot and tasted good. The biscuits were fresh and worked as a good sop. He washed it all down with strong black coffee that must have been brewed yesterday.

"What brings you to Bodie, stranger?" asked Molly.

"I'm looking for an old friend of mine, a guy named Barnes. Runs a store here somewhere."

"Harry Barnes?" she asked.

"Yes, that's him. Know where I can find him?"

"Sure. Step out the front door, look to your right across the field and you'll see the back of his store.

"I heard that Harry's nephew was coming here to go into business with him. Know anything about that?"

"I seen the kid come into town about three days ago. He and his young bride come to set up shop with Harry, so I hear."

Jameson half listened while Molly McGuire rambled on about the lawlessness here in Bodie. About the frequent killings and lack of protection for the decent folks. She and Patrick both wore a side arm at all times but the thugs, as she called them, knew better than mess with Molly. She'd shoot them just as soon as look at them. She figured that as long as they believed that, she was safe.

There used to be 65 saloons here and nearly as many brothels, she said, and the pointed to a framed saying on the wall above the kitchen table. It was a description of Bodie written by the Reverend F. M. Warrington, who said Bodie was "…a sea of sin, lashed by the tempests of lust and passion.

"That's quit a comment on the town. Is it really that bad?"

"Not quite that bad anymore," replied Molly, "but we have had our bad guys. You might have heard of Tom Adams or Washoe Pete?"

"Yes, I've heard the stories but I have never been sure that those guys were real or it was just myths of the Wild West."

"Believe me," said Molly, "they were real, but they're long gone. But we got us another bad man here now, Jake Tibbs. He is as mean and nasty as they come."

"The sheriff in Bridgeport warned me about Tibbs. Isn't there anyone her who can stop Tibbs?"

"The only law around here is in Bridgeport, and if you met the sheriff there, you know he ain't never coming down here, and nobody else wants the kind of trouble Tibbs offers. He's already shot four men this year. He has a few pals that stay close and do his bidding just so they won't be his next victim. He hangs out around King or Bonanza Streets, or at one of the brothels or cribs down near Chinatown. His woman is Lu Wong, works at the Rose Petal. Whore house upstairs, opium den in the back."

"Quite a place, this town of yours, Molly. I'm a peaceful man, myself, so I'll stay away from Tibbs and his ilk, as long as I can. However, I'll level with you, Molly.

There are two more bad guys coming to Bodie and they'll be here soon. They're coming to break up the young Barnes couple who just moved here to work with Harry. They plan to kill young Zach and take Megan back home to her father. They'll probably try to kill me too, when I get in their way."

Jameson went on to describe Scully and Rand, and to advise Molly to stay out of their way.

Are you here to face those two bad guys alone?"

"That's the size of it. But I don't see it as a problem. I've dealt with too many of their kind to worry now."

"You've got grit, I'll give you that. I'll keep an eye open for them coming into town. Let me know if there is anything I can do to help."

"You got it, Molly, Thanks. Otherwise, where can a guy buy a drink without finding trouble as a chaser?"

"There are some nice saloons down on Prospect of King Streets," and she pointed in their direction. There also is a fairly good saloon just up the street, Rondo's. "There are also several decent brothels down around King Street, 'iffen you're are looking for some of that sort of evening?"

"Thanks, Molly. A drink will do nicely. I don't like paying for more than that."

"Sometimes there are more problems come with getting it free than paying for it."

"I think you're right on that. I'll just take in the saloon."

"Depending on which saloon you enter, you might find old Barnes there. He usually spends his evenings, and sometimes his afternoons, in Rondo's, drinking and such. He doesn't mind paying for more than that either."

Jameson finished his soup and coffee, and then walked outside and looked down the street. He heard the usual noises coming from the bars, but the street was clear and he could see that there was no sign of anyone in the *Barnes General Store.*

He ambled down Main Street and turned left on King Street, toward where he could hear some piano music coming from one of the saloons. The name on the window say *Rondo's.* He peered over the swinging saloon doors and liked the looks of it. A few men at the bar drinking and four men at each of two tables playing poker.

Jameson walked in the saloon and went down to the far end where he would have a good view of everyone there or anyone who might come in. The bartender watched him all the way and when Jameson had settled at the end of the bar, he came over,

The bartender looked to be in his sixties. He was lean and gaunt, with sunken cheeks and washed out yellow eyes. His gray hair was long and tied with a red kerchief in a ponytail.

"Welcome to Rondo's, friend. I'm Jimmy Rondo. Name your poison."

"Nice meeting you, Jimmy. My name is Clay, and I'll have a beer and a shot of rye"

"You want me to put the shot of rye in the beer, or do you keep them separate?"

"I'll take them separate. Pouring in the rye is half the fun."

Jimmy Rondo brought Clay his drinks and then stood there, as if he was read to talk."

Jameson poured the shot of rye into his beer and took a drink. "Tell me, Rondo, how is that some of the places around here have electricity?"

"Well, Clay...it is Clay, isn't it?"

"That's right."

"Well, for years the mining mills were powered by steam generated by wood-fired boilers. But eventually the wood supply became scarce and it was getting' more and more costly to transport it in. Based on a theory and lots of hope, last year the mining company here, Standard Company built a hydroelectric plant on Green Creek, above Bridgeport, and strung the wires all the way down here and up to the mills. It worked, as you can see. A few of us were allowed to tap onto the line for a small fee."

"Interesting. I hadn't heard of ever being done."

"It made some history, I guess, 'cause folks from other places came to earn about it and copy it."

While they were talking, two men came through the swinging doors and stood up to the bar. Rondo went down to wait on them. One of them was Zach. Clay recognize him from the photo he had. He was unshaven and looked a little scruffy, from what Clay had expected. The other man was much older and had to be Uncle Harry, from what from what descriptions Clay had been given. He had on soiled overalls, and his torn shirt was hanging out over his hefty gut. His old worn brown cloth hat was slouched to one side and his curly grey hair stuck all around it. An old revolver hung in its holster on his hip.

Rondo brought them each a large glass of beer. They said something by way of a toast, clinked glasses and each took a healthy gulp, then laughed.

Clay took a big drink of his beer, and rise his glass slightly toward Zach and Harry, as if to join in their toast.

Within a few minutes another man entre the saloon and joined Zach and Harry. He raised his right hand, and when Rondo saw him, the man pointed to Zach's beer and pointed a finger in the air to make his order. Rondo understood and brought his beer.

Clay followed the example and when Rondo looked up at him, Clay pointed a finger from each hand, one at the beer glass and one at the empty shoot glass. Rondo was quick to respond with the order.

Clay spoke quietly to the bartender, "Say Rondo, who is that third man who just joined those two at the bar?"

"He's one of the mining engineers. Works for the Standard Company and for one or two of the other mining operations in the area. Nice guy. Quiet. Keeps to himself. No trouble."

Clay looked down the bar at the third guy. Looks young for an engineer, maybe in his late twenties. Tall, lean and muscular. Clean shaven. Blond wavy hair neatly cut and combed. Wears working clothes, but they are clean and look recently pressed. He seemed out of place in a town like Bodie.

The third man was speaking to Zach. "Hey, Zach what are you doing here sopping up that beer. I'd expect you to be home bedding with that young honey of yours. I'll bet she's laying under the covers right now warming it up for you." And he gave Zach's shoulder a gentle hit and laughed.

A smile left Zach's face and he snapped back. "You keep Megan out of your conversation. What she and I do is none of your business. Why don't you take your beer over there," and he pointed to an empty table," and drink with someone who likes you."

"Hey, easy, Zach. I was just busting your chops. I meant no disrespect."

"Well, okay then. Just keep a civil tongue around me."

"Easy, Zach. He meant no harm," said Harry. Anyway, I thought you was going upstairs to one of the rooms. Like I told you, them *femme fatales* like to teach you young newcomers all the latest tricks."

"I might just do that, and I'll teach them a few tricks too." And with that, Zach marched up the stairs to the first room that had a green scarf tied to the door handle and entered. That was the single that the room and girl were available.

Clay decided not to wait around the saloon any longer. He didn't know whether Zach was pushed too far by the engineer and had to prove something or if Zach was planning on going up stirs anyway. Either way, Clay found Zach's behavior disgusting. Not that he cared if a stranger took his personal business up with one of the local whores. It was just that it clashed with the vision he had of Zach and Megan. Two young lovers starting life together. And he agreed with the engineer's comment about why Zach wasn't home with his young honey.

Clay finished his beer and rye blend tipped his hat to Rondo and left the saloon, looking straight ahead out the door.

Outside the sky was so clear that Clay could count every star, or so he thought. He knew that with the sky s clear, the heat was going to rise and it would be cold tonight. It was getting that way already. Tomorrow the sun would have to start warming the day all over again.

He rolled up his collar, stuffed his hands in his front pockets, and walked quickly back to the livery.

Chapter 10

Clay was up early the next morning, washed, dressed and went out to the dining area for breakfast. Molly had prepared steak and eggs, with sourdough biscuits and peach jam. The coffee was fresh.

He waited until mid-morning before going over to the Barnes store. As he entered the front door, he saw Megan Barnes being helped down off a store ladder by that engineer guy he'd seen in the saloon the previous night. The guy's hands were down low on her waist and he held on for several seconds after he had set her on the floor, and then he slid his hands down and across her cheeks as he let her go.

They both saw Jameson at the same time and they parted a respectable distance between themselves as they turned toward him.

Clay glanced quickly around the store. Work clothes, boots, gloves, suspenders, hats, and various styles of shirts were stacked along the shelves. There was also a variety of tools, tack equipment, and camping gear.

"Oh, good morning," said Megan. "I didn't hear you come in. She nodded at the man and said. "He was just helping me down from the ladder." The tone of her voice was almost apologetic.

"Unhuh," responded Jameson.

Megan was a little flustered. She touched her hair and straightened the sales apron she wore. The engineer just stood there with a smile on his face.

"Hello, I'm Megan Barnes. My husband and I are helping his uncle Harry in the store. This is our friend Remy Jones. He helps us too, from time to time."

Megan approached Jameson, as she introduced herself, and she and Jameson shook hands.

"I'm Clay Jameson, Mrs. Barnes." And he quickly turned to face the engineer.

"Remy? That's your name, Remy?"

"Yes. It's short for Remington. Is that a problem for you?" Remy responded in a questioning tone that took on a hard edge as he spoke.

"No, Remy. No problem for me. It's your name. Now if it was my name, then it might be a problem." He had a wry smile on his face as he addressed Remy.

Both he and Megan waited for Remy's reply and were just a little uncertain as to how he would take Jameson's comments.

Remy paused for a few seconds and then said, "Hey, I don't blame you a minute. Why if your name was Remy, then who would I be?" Then his face broke out in a big grin.

Jameson laughed, and they shook hands, each showing good natured grins. They each also displayed a strong grip to each other, as men sometimes are wont to do.

"How may I help you Mr. Jameson," asked Megan.

"Actually, Mrs. Barnes, I am here to help you. I need some time to talk with you and Zach."

"Well what is it, Mr. Jameson. My husband is not here right now," and she took a quick look at Remy, "but you can tell me and I'll convey it to my husband."

"It's personal and private, and I need to speak to both of you at the same time."

"I better leave Meg... er... Mrs. Barnes."

"You needn't go, Remy." Responded Megan, in what sounded like a challenge to Jameson's request.

"Yes, Remy you need to go." Countered Clay. "And maybe you can tell Zach and Uncle Harry that I need to speak to them, now."

"I don't think I like your tone Mr. Jameson," Megan replied.

"I'm not here for that, Mrs. Barnes. I'm here to talk to you."

Megan was flustered. She didn't know how to respond to Jameson's retort.

Jameson looked at Remy again and said, "We'll see you later, I supposed, and I would appreciate it if you would tell Zach and Harry to get over here."

Remy gave a half salute as a sarcastic gesture that he understood the command and would obey, and he left.

Megan stood tall with her arms folded in front of her, and with a demanding look on her face.

"Megan, and I would like to call you Megan instead of Mrs. Barnes. I came here from Andersville for find you."

Megan put her right hand over her mouth, and then asked, "What do you mean you came here to find me."

"Actually, your father hired me to find you, but I am here as a friend, and I'm here to help you."

"But I don't need any help, thank you, so you can go right back to my father and tell him you found me and I don't need your help or anyone's help"

"Yes, Megan I'm afraid you do. If we could wait a few minutes, I would like to tell you and Zach at the same time, that is if Remy can find Zach."

"Oh, he'll find Zach alright, but I'm not certain that he will convince him to come back here."

"Zach getting a little independent lately,' quipped Jameson.

"You could say that," Megan replied.

"I saw he down at Rondo's saloon last night. What time did he come home?"

"It was after two…that's not your concern."

"I think it is, Megan, but we'll go into that later."

Just then Remy came back with Zach and Harry in tow. "Here they are, Clay. Just like the doctor ordered."

"Thanks, Remy, we'll catch you up later." And Jameson just stood there waiting for Remy to leave. Remy understood and after a fleeting glance at Megan, he left. Jameson thought he saw Megan nod her head ever so slightly to Remy during that quick glance.

It might have been better to let Remy stay and hear it all. They might need his help if and when Scully and Rand appear. Megan might have wanted Remi to stay, but Zach probably would not.

Harry looked at Jameson and said, "What's this all about? You interrupted our lunch."

"Zach...Harry, my name is Clay Jameson. Here's my card." And Clay handed all three of them his business card. I was hired by Mr. Williams, Megan's father, to find you, Zach and Megan, and see that you are alright. He hoped that by this time Megan would realize the mistake she made in getting married and would want to come home."

"You've got your nerve," responded Zach. "Of course, we're alright, and no one wants to come home. We don't need your help and we don't want you here, so get your ass out of here and leave us alone." Zach spoke in a demanding tone and took a step or two toward Jameson.

Megan seemed surprised at Zach's reaction. She had not seen him so demonstrative before and even smiled at watching him being assertive.

Jameson took a deep breath and kept his manner

calm and collected, although he would have preferred to get right in Zach's face. "I'm not through explaining the situation. And yes, Zach, you do need my help. Let's all sit down and hear me out before you start running off at the mouth." And Jameson turned his back on the three walked over to the stove in the far wall and sat down in one of the several chairs placed around the rail in front of the stove.

The other stood their place momentarily, as if they weren't sure how to react. Then Megan said, "Okay, you've come all this way to find us, Mr. Jameson, so the least we can do is hear you out." And she walked over and took a chair opposite Jameson.

Zach and Harry hesitated for a moment, but then followed Megan and took chairs on either side of her and across from Jameson.

"Like I said, Megan your father is unhappy that you married Zach and wants you to come home. However, he hopes that Zach doesn't come home. Zach your parents are anxious about how you two are getting on and they are worried about you coming to a place like Bodie. Now, that's the good news."

"What do you mean, *that's the good news?*" interrupted Megan. "What did he expect Zach to do?"

"I don't think he cared what Zach does, as long as he didn't come back with you,"

"Tell me, Mr. Jameson, if that's the good news, what's the bad news."

"Call me Clay,"

"What?"

"Clay. I'd like you all to call me Clay, since we are going to be working closely together until the situation is resolved."

"Alright, Clay," continued Harry, "what's the bad news?"

All three of them leaned a little closer toward Clay as he was ready to speak.

"Megan's father has two ranch hands, John Scully and Rand Gomez."

"They're not ranch hands," interjected Megan, expressing the disgust she had for them. "They're his hired guns. They do his dirty work."

"That's right, Megan. That's exactly the point I'm getting to. I got the distinct impression that your father wasn't happy with the fact that I told him that I wouldn't kill Zach and that I would only help you as you wanted it to be. So, he sent Scully and Rand to follow me and do the *dirty work*, as you called it."

Megan and Zach sat back in their chairs, with an expression of surprise mixed with fear. Harry just looked angry.

"You mean that they are somewhere out there right now looking to jump us?" asked Zach.

"I did my best not to let them know which way I went or where I was going, but I have the feeling that Scully is smart enough to find out. He might even have pressured your parents, Zach, into telling what knew. And they knew I was coming here."

Zach cringed slightly, Megan sat up straight and look determined, and Harry continued to look angry.

"So, Clay," asked Megan," what do you propose?"

"At some point there is going to be a fight. I had a nice talk with the sheriff in Bridgeport and he is going to be on the lookout for those two. He might arrest them and wait for us or me to come back. Or, he might tell them where I went and send them on. Or, he might not do anything. He wants to avoid dealing or even finding problems. So, we need to keep and constant eye for them over the next few days, and stay close and be ready if trouble comes.'

"Let them come. I ready for those skunks anytime they want, to come and get it" boasted Harry. And he proudly patted the revolver in his holster.

Harry carried a Colt 1851 Navy Model .36 caliber cap and ball revolver. A little underpowered for today's use, and slow to load. And he probably hadn't fired it in years. Remy, on the other hand had a Smith and Wesson 1878 chambered for the .44 Russian, a fine piece.

"We need to work out some plans," stated Megan, "and be ready for whatever comes."

"I need and drink," said Zach, and he stood up. "Come on, Harry. Let's me and you get a drink and we'll work out our own plan." Zach walked toward the door and Harry followed.

"Zach," called Megan, "weren't you listening?? You can't just..." and she let her voice trail off as Zach walked out of the store.

Clay recognized that Megan was upset and concerned over much more than just the thought of Scully and Rand. Something went missing in the relationship she and Zach had.

"When did Zach take to drinking, Megan?"

"It started the day after we arrived here. It's Harry. His uncle Harry just sucked him up and is dragging him down to his own level. I don't understand, and I don't know what to do." And her eyes filled with tears, and she reached out to be hugged by Clay. Even though she had just met him, Megan sensed Clay's concern and felt his compassion. She felt as if she had known him and trusted him forever.

Clay held her for a good long minute and let Megan cry it out. When her crying stopped, she looked up at his face and said, "Thanks, I guess I needed that." They smiled at each other.

Megan notice a small scar on the lower portion of his left cheek which didn't seem noticeable until he smiled. She gently touched his cheek and the scar. "Oh, where did you get that scar?"

"It's a long story,"" Clay replied. "I was living with a small tribe of Paiute Indians around Lovelock, Nevăda for a few months about four years ago. I was trying to learn their language and, for a while they were very friendly. Then the practice of a ritual called the Ghost Dance spread to the tribe from the Lakota's. It was a dance in a large circle that they believed would connect them with their spirit ancestors, and would also drive out the white man. One of their young braves took it seriously and challenged me to a fight. He nicked me with his knife during the fight before I hit him along side of his head with the heavy butt of my knife, and he fell to the ground, unconscious. The rest of the tribe saw me as the winner and honored me as a great fighter. I saddled my horse and left the tribe before that brave woke up."

"My, Mr. Jameson, it sounds as though you have had some adventures in your life."

"A few, Megan, a few"

Megan and clay were still standing close, and she was still drying her eyes when the door opened and Remy walked into the store.

Remy realized that he had interrupted something, but he wasn't sure what that something was so he said, "hope I'm not interrupting anything."

Megan stepped back from Clay, wiped the remaining tears from her face and looked toward Remy, and then back at Clay, as if she was asking him for permission to let Remy stay.

"Come in, Remi," Clay said in a positive and clear tone. "I think that you are needed at a time like this. We probably should have let you stay before, but I wasn't sure."

"And you're sure now?" asked Remi.

"Yes, I'm sure. I think we need another man here."

Remy walked over to where Clay and Megan were standing. He looked back and forth between them, questioning them with his eyes. Megan turned to face him, and started to lift her arms,

"Remy," said Clay, I think she need another hug."

They embraced, and Remy seemed a little awkward, as if not fully understanding the situation... Megan looked up and over at Clay and gave him a sweet and knowing smile, as if to say, *thanks, you understand*. Then they stepped apart and Remy looked over to Clay.

Clay pointed to the chairs by stove and said, "I think if we sat down Remy, we have some explaining to do. But first, let me make one thing clear. I am assuming from all that I have seen from you that you are here to help Megan. If that's not the case, and if you are here on a lark or because you have nothing better to do with your time, you better leave now. Because, Remy, when we are finished talking here, you will be committed to risk your feelings, and maybe your life to help her."

"Clay, I have never before been committed to anything beyond my own satisfactions and needs, but let me assure you, I am with you all the way. I am with Megan all the way, whatever the risk."

A warm feeling ran through Megan's body and she beamed a smiled to both of them. "Clay, she said," I feel that we are going to make it. Whatever we need to do to resolve this situation, we can't miss, with the two of you feeling as you do."

Clay explained the entire scenario to Remy, and Megan added her thoughts as well. He described Scully and Rand Gomez and stressed the aggression they would face.

Finally, Remy, took in a deep breath and said, "You mean that these two thugs might or might not come here and if they get here, they will try to kill Zach and take Megan back home?"

"That's the size of it.'

"It ain't going to happen, Clay. It's just not going to happen."

"We're thankful for your support, Remy. We know that they are looking for Megan, but we don't know for certain that they will come here. I hope that they do, and we can be ready for them. If they don't get here, we know that they will be out there somewhere looking. We'll give it two more days to expect them here. If they don't come, I'll start back and find them and settle it."

"So how do you want to handle this?" asked Remy.

"I'm glad you asked, because everyone must understand that I am in charge. This sort of situation falls often within the business I do. First of all, I am going to find Zach and Harry, jerk them up and make them realize what is at stake here. We can all get together here and work out our strategy. Remy, you stay here for a few minutes with Megan. I'll get the other two and be back soon,"

Clay started for the door, then half way there he turned toward Remy and said, "Remy, step outside with me for a minute, would you. Something I wanted to ask you."

"Sure thing, Clay," and they walked outside and shut the door, but stood in the doorway talking.

Clay said, "Remy, I'm not one to mince words and I don't want any false lines coming back my way. I want to know exactly what's going on between you and Megan and what your intentions are, and what's happening with Zach,"

Remy hesitated momentarily and looked at Clay, and then said, "I met Megan the first day they arrived. I was helping Harry and Zach unload their wagon. I had a hard time keeping my eyes off of her, she's so beautiful, and then over the last two days I've found that she is bright, warm and kind, and I guess that my lust just moved on into love. I have respected Zach and their marriage, and haven't made any overt moves, but when I am with her, I know that she senses how I feel and that she feels the same way. It's been real hard keeping my hands off of her, when I want to take her in my arms and sweep her away from here, and say to hell with Zach."

"Does Zach know how you feel?"

"I don't think so. Ever since they arrived, he has been spellbound by Harry's talk and leading him on to drink with him and be one of the boys. I think he's even gone to the brothels at Harry's goading, leaving Megan with nothing. I can't understand how she ever agreed to marry him. It seems like there is nothing between them now."

"So, feeling that way, what do you plan to do about it?"

"When this situation is over and everyone is in the clear, I'm going to tell Megan how I feel and then, depending upon what she says, I'm hoping that we'll tell Zach and see what happens."

"Remy, thanks for your honesty. I can appreciate just how you feel. She is all that you say she is and more, and I am working to accomplish whatever makes her safe and happy. I'm think that maybe Zach is having growing pains, overwhelmed by the sudden responsibility of marriage and standing on his own two feet. This situation we're facing might shake some sense and responsibility in him."

"You can count on me for anything we need to do here. You might be right about Zach, but I doubt it."

"Okay, Remy, enough said. You get back inside and watch for our scruffy friends. I'll see what I can do with Zach and Harry."

As Clay walked away from the store, he reflected on what Remy had said. Clay was as suspicious man. It was not that he didn't trust people. He neither trusted nor distrusted. He merely suspended the need to call it either way at the beginning and he would let it play out to see which way it fell at the end.

Clay thought that Remy's responses came too quickly and were too positive and complete. He was too ready with the answer, but who could argue with what he said. It was the nice thing to say. The right thing. Remy's ardor seemed to blossom rather quickly, however. And yet, Clay sensed that Megan had similar feelings. Time will tell, and Clay would stay alert to know. Right now, the focus had to be on preparing for Scully and Rand.

Chapter 11

Remy re-entered the store. Megan was standing where he had left her.

"Megan, are you alright?"

"As much as anyone could be, given the situation we're in," she replied. "I'm so glad that you stayed and offered to help."

"I wouldn't have it any other way, Megan. I care for you a great deal."

"I know. That's one of the aspects of the situation that adds to my confusion and one that I know I must deal with when things with Scully and Rand are settled."

"I don't understand what Scully and Rand are doing here. Why would your father send them? What does he want?"

Megan decided to confide completely in Remy, "Whether you know it or not, my father runs a vast business empire, with shipping, cattle, and land development. What he wants is a responsible man to run that business after he retires. I had two brothers whom my father had hoped that one day would share the reins, but one ran off and other either drown or ran off as well. I told him that I could run the business as good as anyone, but he insists that a man take over. And not just any man. He wanted me to marry a man of his choice, one who he can bully around just as he does everyone. Well, I didn't want to marry one of his choosing. It's my life and I'll do the choosing."

"So, you chose Zach? What, to spite your father or because you loved him?"

"At the time, I thought we loved each other and that we would build a new and wonderful life together. But now I don't know. Maybe I did want to spite father, or maybe I just wanted to get away. It's all mixed up now, and our new life together isn't going as I planned. This place is horrible, Uncle Harry is debauching old slob, good for nothing but drinking and whoring, and he seems to be converting Zach to his way of life. I feel trapped, Remy, with no way out and powerless to change things."

"You're not helpless, Megan. You know what you want and you have people to help you. Just follow your heart, follow your instincts. I'll help you get what you want."

"Oh Remy, I know that you are there for me, and I feel so good that you are, but too much is going on right now. I've got to sort it all out, and we all have to face Scully and Rand before I can think any further."

Remy moved toward Megan, as if to embrace her, but she held up a hand and said, "Not now Remy. I can't right now."

Scully and Rand walked out the sheriff's office in Bridgeport, after spending the night in jail. The sheriff had kept a hundred dollars that Scully had left over from what Williams had given him. The sheriff also had acknowledged that he knew that they were after Zach and Megan Barnes, and probably Jameson as well.

The sheriff had made it clear that he would not stand for any trouble in Bridgeport. That if trouble was to happen, they had better start and finish it is Bodie. He also insisted on their word that Megan would not be harmed, but only taken back home. What happened to Zach was between them. Western tradition still held onto the belief that a man had better take care of himself, but no harm should come to a woman.

"Well, at least we know where they are and that Jameson is there too," said Scully.

"So how do you want to handle it? Replied Rand.

"We'll camp just this side of Bodie tonight and go into town at first light. We get Jameson first. Shoot him on sight. From what the sheriff told us about Bodie, we can figure that no one will care or get in our way. After that, Zach will be a cinch. Then we'll grab the girl up and tie her up in that wagon they came in and take her home."

"John?"

"Yeah?"

"On the way home, can I take her, you know?"

"We'll see how it goes, Rand. She might be willing by that time, but we can't take a chance on harming her or old Williams will fire us for sure."

"Okay, John, but I sure would like to have that pretty young thing, just once. Show her she ain't as uppity as she pretends."

Rand was almost salivating, dreaming of bedding the Williams girl. He might even get to have her more than once. He might even get rid of Scully somewhere on the way home. He was tired of doing as he was told by Scully. Then he could have the girl as often as he wanted, and he wouldn't take her home. He'd just finish her off and leave the area.

Scully was thinking that they'd find a quiet spot on the way home and he tell Rand to have her, but then Scully would step in, as if to save her. He'd shoot Rand and take the Williams girl home. He bet he would be rewarded well by Williams.

Clay walked up the street to Rondo's saloon, where he hoped to find Zach and Harry. As he entered, he saw them standing at the bar sipping a beer. He walked up to the bar next to Zach, took him by the elbow and said, "Zach come over to the table with me. I need to talk to you for a few minutes. Harry, you can stay here and mind the bar."

Just as Clay was turning to led Zach across the saloon floor to one of the tables, Jake Tibbs walked in the door. "Hey you motley bunch of drifters, Jake is here, "he yelled. "Drinks are on me. Everyone to the bar."

Clay held on to Zach's arm and again started leading him to one of the tables. Tibbs stepped in front of them and said, "I said up to the bar. Jake's buying and when I say up to the bar, I mean everyone."

Tibbs was a tall and rotund man, with a mop of dirty red hair, and a splotchy red and grey full beard. He wore denim bib overalls and a red and black checked wool shirt over his long john upper. He looked and smelled as though he hadn't bathed or washed his clothes for weeks.

Tibbs looked over to Zach and said, "Hey kid. Tell your dumb friend here that people around this place do what Jake says to do.

No one saw Clay straighten and stiffen the forefinger on his right hand. And later, no one could say that they saw Clay jab Tibbs in his stomach. All people could recall was that suddenly Tibbs let out all his wind, with an accompanying gasp, grab his stomach and double up on the floor. No one saw that as he was falling, Clay snatched Tibbs revolver from his holster and shove it into his own waist band.

"What happened," Someone asked. "Jake, what's wrong."

Clay responded, "I think he just lost his breath. He'll be alright in a minute." The Clay led Zach over to a table and the both sat.

"Zach, I need your attention now. Are you listening?"

"What do you want? Why are you bothering us?"

Zach seemed not to comprehend, and Clay slapped

him across the face. "Do I have your attention?"

"Yes… okay. I'm listening."

"Zach, what happened? The two of you left town in such wedded bliss and set out to make your own life, starting here in Bodie helping Uncle Harry. What went wrong?"

"I can't say completely. We started out fine. She was good at loving, and she seemed so supportive. But when we got here, she started taking over, running the store. Telling me and Harry what to do, and what not to do. It was going to be me and Harry, and then she took over. I don't know how it happened, but I couldn't put up with it so me and Harry would just leave and get a beer. It seemed the easiest way. Now I don't know where we are."

"And do you realize, Zach, that Scully and Rand are coming here to take Megan home, and that they will kill you in the process?"

"Why would they want to kill me? I ain't done nothing to them or to Mr. Williams."

"Yes, you have Zach. You married his daughter and run off with her. He expected her to marry someone who could take over his business affairs when he retires. You weren't that someone. He figured that the only way to get her back was to get you out of the picture. They are mean guys, and you are either going to have to fight them and win or die."

"I'm thinking, now, Clay, with things the way they are, that if I just let them have her, she can go back with them and I'll stay here with Harry."

Clay wanted to slap Zach around until he came to his senses, but he realized that Zach might not come around. Clay looked at Zach with both disgust and pity. What a poor excuse for a man.

Clay noticed that Tibbs was standing now and seemed to have regained his breathing and composure. He didn't even realize that Clay had taken his stiff first finger and shoved it very hard and very quick into Tibbs solar plexus, nocking all the breath out of Tibbs.

Tibbs was looking around the saloon and spotted Clay and walked over to the table where Clay and Zach were sitting. "Hey, mister, what did you do to me back there? All of a sudden I couldn't breathe and thought I was going to die.'

"I didn't do anything, Jake. We were talking and you suddenly grabbed you stomach, heaved out some air and fell to your knees."

Jake was looking befuddled, like he should know what happened and can't understand why he doesn't.

"Someone over at the bar said you had my gun. I want it back."

"Sure, Jake. It looks as though it was jabbing you in the side as you doubled up so I took it to hold it for you, Here." And Clay handed Jake his revolver, but he had unloaded it first, just in case Jake planned to use it on Clay.

Tibbs took his gun and holstered it without noticing that it was empty. "Well, thanks.,,a,,,what's your name?"

"It's Clay, Jake. Clay Jameson."

"Well, okay, Clay…a…thanks." And Tibbs walked back to the bar.

"Zach, you can let Megan go back with Scully and Rand, but there is no guarantee that they won't abuse her on the way, and they were paid to take you out, not to leave you here. They're going to kill you Zach, unless you do exactly what I say and you allow Remy and me to handle this on our terms. Afterwards, you can do what you want, and Megan can either stay or leave."

"You really mean that Scully and Rand are just going to come into Bodie and shoot me. Isn't there any law her or somebody that protects people here?"

"No law, and no protection beyond what you can do for yourself. Unless you do exactly what I say."

Zach just sat there for a few minutes mulling over his situation and trying to make sense of it. "Okay, Clay. What do you want me to do?"

"You need to come back to the store with me, and you, Remy and Megan will work out a strategy to follow for the next two days, at the most. After that, I will assume that Scully and Rand and either back in Bridgeport in jail or are still looking for me. I'll go back and find them and settle it."

"What about Harry?" asked Zach.

Just then Harry came staggering toward the table. He had been drinking with Tibbs while Zach and Clay were talking. He was drunk.

"Sit down, Harry," offered Clay. Zach and I were just about to leave and go back to the store so we can plan a way to take care of Scully and Rand before they kill Zach. You bet stay here and watch for them. I'll fill I you in on what to do if we need your help."

Clay had decided to keep Harry out of it. He would just get in the way and probably get himself killed.

"Okay, Clay. That's nice. I'll stay right here." Harry was too drunk now to even understand what we were up against.

"Zach, we're going back to the store now. I left Remy there to protect Megan while I came to find you. When we get back there, Remy and I are going to step outside for a few minutes. While we're gone, you need to convince Megan that you're sorry for being such an ass, and that we are in this together."

With that, Clay and Zach walked out of the saloon, leaving Harry slouched over the table and Tibbs drinking at the bar.

Chapter 12

Clay and Zach entered the Barnes store. Megan was working behind the counter and Remy was sitting near the stove.

"How is everything here?" asked Clay.

"Things are about the same," replied Remy. Megan looked up at Zach and then walked in the back, into a room that had been converted into their bedroom. Harry slept in a loft room.

Clay motioned to Remy to follow him out the door and that they were leaving. He motioned to Zach to go to Megan.

Megan was sitting on the edge of the bed when Zach walked into the room. "Megan, I'm sorry about the way I've been acting. I'm not meaning to hurt you. I just feel overwhelmed and everything is out of hand. I didn't know it would be like this, being out on our own. You seem to be taking it all in stride, but I don't know how to respond."

Megan had time to think it all over and she knew what she wanted and what she didn't want. Remy's words had given her the courage to act.

"Zach, I know that you didn't mean to hurt me. You didn't mean to do anything. That's part of the problem. We both expected life to be different, and we both wanted something different out of our marriage and our trip to Bodie. I think we both married for the wrong reasons, but neither of us knew it at the time. We've changed, Zach. Bodie has changed us. I have a much clearer idea of what I want out of life now, and it doesn't include Bodie. We were bound *for* Bodie when we started, but we're not bound *to* Bodie now. I'm leaving, Zach as soon as this mess with Scully and Rand is settled. I'm sorry, Zach, but I can't live like this. I need more out of life. You do what you have to do. That's the way is going to be."

They were both teary eyed by now and they rose to face each other. Megan went over to Zach and gave him a hug. He hugged her in return, and they held each other for a long few seconds. They both realized that this was best and they both felt relieved now that it had be said.

Zach was thinking that if she leaves, he'd be free to stay here with Harry and have some fun out of life. He was feeling that he had been made to carry Christ in his heart every day and to stifle any urges that he felt. Now he was like a kid away from for the first time, and he was enjoying all the debauchery he could get.

Megan was feeling glad that the opportunity had presented itself for her to speak her mind and take a stand against staying in Bodie. If Zach stayed here, she would return home and obtain an annulment or a divorce, whatever it took, and start her life in a more positive direction, one in which she was in charge.

Outside the store Clay and Remy scanned the streets looking for signs of Scully and or Rand. Clay wished they would come. It would be easier settling things here in town and with Remy's help.

"What do you suppose they are talking about, Clay?"

"I trust that it's about them, and their relationship, such as it is. Did you say anything to her about it?"

"Yes, I did clay. And I told her just how I felt too. This whole ordeal puts a lot of pressure on Megan. She's the one who will decide. Zach is not up to it."

"Just don't mess with her, Remy. I don't want her hurt anymore."

"You got some thoughts about her for yourself, Clay?"

'No Remy. I can't get involved in anything like this. I was hired to do a job and I always go beyond what is just necessary to be sure any job I take is complete. All I have is my reputation."

"I hear you, Clay. I won't do anything to hurt Megan. I'm hoping to make her mine someday."

"Well, you might become a couple someday, but she's never going to belong to you or anyone. She's never be anyone's property."

Clay and Remy saw that Zach and Megan were back in the main part of the story, so they went back inside.

Clay looked at Remy and asked, "Where are you staying at night?"

"I have a room directly across the street from the store, at the Miner's Inn. I have an upstairs front room, and I can watch the entire store and surrounding streets. You?

"I have a room at the McGuire Livery Stable. They gave me an upstairs room above their living area, but I will move into a portion of Harry's small livery stable behind the store. We'll have it covered from both ends."

Clay looked at Megan and Zach. "When we aren't here for any reason, you two keep the doors locked and' stay out of sight. We'll spend most of the time here, and if we leave, we won't be far away."

Megan rose and spoke to all of them, "I'll fix us some lunch. You three relax if you can. This is going to be an anxious wait." And she went back into the kitchen.

After lunch, took their chairs up near the front window and sat there scanning the street and watching the people who walked by. There weren't very many.

Megan sat at a small desk behind the counter and began writing a letter to her parents. She planned to mail it on her way home once they were able to leave Bodie.

Zach paced the floor around the stove and walked to the window a few times. "I'm worried about Uncle Harry," he said to whomever was listening. He should be back by now. I think I'll go up to Rondo's saloon and get him."

"Zach..." began Megan, but Zach stopped her.

"It's okay, Megan. I'll be careful. Uncle Harry might need some help to get home. I'll be right back."

And with that, Zach walked out the door and up the street.

Clay was going to stop him, but decided it was better to keep Zach occupied than having him sit around here and bother everyone with his pacing. He and Remy would watch for any signs of anyone coming into town.

Zach entered the saloon and saw Harry sitting at the same table where they left him. He was sitting up and alert, and was sipping a beer. Zach decided to join him. One beer won't hurt.

Harry was glad to see him, "Zach, where you been. I was about to come looking for you. I must have fallen asleep earlier, but I feel fine now."

The bartender brought Zach a beer, and he lifted in toast to Harry. I'm here now Uncle Harry."

Just then Jake Tibbs strolled into the saloon.
He was relatively quiet and looked as though he had just woken up. He ordered a beer and began talking to one of his cronies at the far end of bar.

Harry turned toward Zach with a quick gesture and a smile from ear to ear. He looked like the cat who was going to swallow the canary. "Zach, I just got the greatest idea," he said in a quiet voice, almost a whisper. "Finish that beer quickly and follow me."

"What, Uncle Harry" What are we going to do?"

"Shush!" said Harry. "Just follow me."

They both finished their beers and Zach followed Harry out the door and down the street to the right, toward Chinatown.

"Uncle Harry, where're going?"

"Keep on waking, son. You know that place that Tibbs always goes, the Rose Petal?"

"Yeah!"

"Well I have been looking for a way to show up old Tibbs, and seeing as how he just came into the saloon, he'll be there for a while, and seeing as how you 're here, you can do the deed."

"What do you mean, do the deed?"

"I'm going to show you heaven on earth, my boy. You're going be pleasured like you have never had it before. We are going to see Lu Wong, Tibbs woman, and she is going to teach you the mysteries of the orient."

"Oh, I don't know, Uncle Harry. I should get back to the store. I told Megan…"

"Tut, tut, tut, my boy," interrupted Harry. Never you mid about that. Ah, here we are, the Rose Petal." And Harry opened the front door and led Zach inside.

They were met by a small framed middle-aged Chinese man, who bowed and welcomed them. "What can we do for you today, Harry?"

"Hello, Ben. This here's my nephew, Zach. He's new in town and I want him to be introduced to one of Bodie's rich tapestries. We want to see Lu Wong."

"I'll see if she is available," he replied.

Just then a voice from the second floor called over the railing. "Of course, I am available. Did I hear right, Harry, you brought that young man to see me?"

"I give you the boy, Lu Wong. Send me back a man."

Lu Wong was walking down the stairs at a slow pace, wearing a long red silken robe, which she let fall open here and there as she descended. Zach stared at the way she moved as she came down the stairs.

She reached out her hand and Zach took it. She began leading him up the stairs at the same slow pace. "Zach, is it, we are going to Shangri-La, where all the pleasures of the Orient reside, and you will never want to return."

They disappeared upstairs and around the corner into the front bedroom. Harry nodded to old ben, and then seated himself on one of the two chairs in the foyer.

Harry had been sitting there for only about ten minutes when the front door swung open and there stood Jake Tibbs. Harry recoiled at the sight.

"Where's Lu Wong?" he demanded. He looked at Harry. Where is that runt nephew of yours?" Is he up with my woman?"

"Now Jake," began Harry, and he rose to stand between Tibbs and the stairway. Tibbs gave Harry a brutal shove, and he fell back onto the sofa, and then bounced onto the floor.

Tibbs lumbered up the stairs and kicked open the door to Lu Wong's room. She was straddling Zach and they were both naked on the bed. She looked to the door as it was flung open and she saw the anger in Tibbs eyes. She let out a little shriek and tried to get off of the bed.

Jake Tibbs grabbed Lu Wong by the hair on her head and yanked her off of Zach and threw her to the floor, and kicked her in the stomach.

Zach wasn't sure what was going to happen, but he knew he had better get out of there. He started to rise from the bed, but Tibbs put his huge right hand behind Zach's neck and flung him against the wall near the window.

Tibbs was seething now and drooling like an enraged bull. "You don't fuck my woman. She is my woman. You stand up."

Zack rose to his feet, leaning against the wall, and curling his arms around his chest. There was terror in his eyes. "I didn't know she was your, Jake. I didn't know."

"I teach you not to fuck my woman." And Tibbs drew his pistol from his holster and shot Zach right between his legs, blasting off his penis and testicles all over the wall behind him.

Zach let out a moan that began in a low sub-human tone and increased in pitch to a horrible cry of wounded animal. His face was white and his eyes were wide open, as if in disbelief.

"Shut up, you little prick. You don't ever fuck with my woman," and Tibbs shot Zach again right through the heart.

Then Tibbs opened the window all the way, grabbed Zach by the nape of his neck, drug him to the window, and through him to the ground below.

Lu Wong cowered in a corner, covered with her robe. She had seen Jake get angry, but never like this. She was afraid of what he might do to her.

Tibbs looked over at Ku Wong, and said, "You don't never fuck nobody but me ever again." And he walked toward her and appeared to be getting ready to kick her.

"I won't Jake. I'm your woman, forever. Please Jake."

Tibbs gave her a long look of contempt and let out a sound of disgust. "Next time I catch you with another man I kill you too."

"I won't Jake. I promise. I'm your woman."

Zach lay sprawled on the ground in front of the Rose Petal. The life gone out of him. Harry had heard the shots and seen a body fall from the window above. He ran outside and found Zach. He couldn't believe what had happened and first. Finally, Harry knelt down and lifted Zach's head into his arms. He began to cry.

"I'm sorry Zach. I didn't know. I didn't know."

Suddenly he heard a voice from the window above. It was Jake laughing and saying, "See, I teach him to fuck my woman."

The rage welled up within Harry beyond control. It was compelled by a mixture of guilt and hate. "Why you bastard, Jake. You didn't have to kill him."

Harry drew his old cap and ball pistol from his holster and fired at Jake. His shot missed by two feet. Jake pulled his pistol, laughed, and shot down at Harry, hitting him in the chest. He stumbled and fell, and Jake shot him two more times. He was dead.

Jake looked back at Lu Wong again. We won't be bothered by those two again. I'll be back in an hour or so. You better be here, and alone."

"Sure, Jake. I will."

Tibbs walked down stairs and out the door and up the street toward Rondo's Saloon. He glanced down at Zach and Harry as he walked passed them. "Yeah, I teach you. Both of you."

Chapter 13

Megan paced back and forth in the store. She was concerned that Zach hadn't returned. Remy was dozing in a chair sitting by the front window, and Clay was pacing by the front door. He was just about ready to leave and search for Zach when a man walked up to the door and tried the knob.

The door was locked. Clay looked at the man, who was dressed in work clothes and was carrying a lunch pail. Clay opened the door. "Come on in. We're not officially open, but maybe we can help you."

He entered and looked at the three of them. "My name is Dobbs, Gordon Dobbs." He looked over to Megan. "Ma'am, remember me. I was in yesterday and bought some stuff from that young nephew of Harry's., Zach. I guess he was your husband."

"Yes, Mr. Dobbs, I do remember. These are our friends, Clay Jameson and Remy Jones. What can we do for you?"

"I got some bad news, ma'am. It's about Zach, and

about Harry too. I hate to tell you ma'am, but they're dead."

They all went into some form of shock, but Megan looked as though she was going to pass out. Clay went to her quickly, and led her to one of the chairs by the stove, and helped to her to sit.

"Gordon, can you come over here. We all need to hear the details." And Clay directed everyone to take a chair. He sat next to Megan and put his arm arounds her shoulder to comfort her.

"Tell us everything that you know about what happened, Gordon?"

"Well, I was walking down the hill from my shift at the mine. I cut through Chinatown because it more direct to my house. As I neared King Street, I heard a shot, then there was a pause, then another shot. It sounded like pistol shot to me. As I neared the Rose Pearl this guy came flying out of an upstairs window and flopped on the ground. Then Harry came running out, looked at the body and tried to cradle the head in his arms. Then I saw Jake Tibbs appear at the window and yell down at Harry. Harry stood up and yelled something back at Tibbs, and then drew his pistol and shot at Tibbs. He missed, and then Tibbs shot back from the window and hit Harry. Shot him three times. Then Tibbs came out the brothel door and I seen him walk up toward the Rondo Saloon. I stayed to see what I could do to help."

No one said a word. All three just sat there and looked at Dobbs. Megan had her hands held to her face, as if in horror, but she had a completely blank expression on her face.

Finally, Clay said, "Where are the bodies now, Gordon."

"Henry Stokes, the undertaker was there in about five minutes. He usually keeps a horse and wagon hitched, ready for business, and when he hears shooting, he comes there. He said he would take the bodies to his place, then I said I would come and tell you. I'm just awful sorry Mrs. Barnes."

Megan just looked at Dobbs, nodded her head and gave a half smile.

"Gordon," stated Clay, "will you go see Mr. Stokes and ask him to clean up the bodies and put them in plain wooden caskets? We'll come there in a little while."

"Sure. Mr. Jameson. That's the least I can do." And Dobbs left the store.

Clay looked at Remy. "You stay here with Megan. I'm going to settle the score with Tibbs. I'll be back soon."

"Clay, let me…"

"No, Remy. That one is on me. You stay here. Megan is going to need all the support we can give her. Not to worry. I'll be back soon."

Clay picked up his 12-guage shotgun that he had leaned against the wall in the corner. He checked to be sure it was fully loaded, with one ready to fire, and left for Rondo's Saloon.

Clay walked down to the Rondo and stood in front of the Saloon door, raised the shotgun waist high and held it in his right hand, and then pulled a small .38 cal. derringer from his pocket and held it in his left hand, and then entered the saloon. Six or seven men were standing at the bar drinking and several more men sat around the four tables located opposite the bar area.

Clay saw Tibbs standing two thirds of the way down the bar talking with two friends. No one noticed Clay at first. He pointed the derringer at the ceiling above him and fired one shot. The room went completely quiet and all the men jumped and turned toward him. He shoved the derringer in his pocket and raised the shotgun waist high and held it with both hands. He right index finger laying alongside the trigger guard.

Now that he had everyone's attention he yelled, "Tibbs, you son-of-a –bitch, I'm calling you out."

Tibbs stood where he was against the bar. The two men next to him moved quickly to the other side of the bar.

"I'm here just for Tibbs, so the rest of you gents can relax. But if I see anyone moving their hand toward their holster, I'll shoot him. You, behind the bar, move up here to the front of the bar, away from Tibbs. And if you move toward a gun, you're dead."

"I ain't got no gun, mister. I don't want no trouble," said the bartender.

"Everyone else better stay to the far right of the room, away from Tibbs. This riot gun is a 12-guage holds five shots and has a wide shot spread."

"What do you want with me," asked Tibbs. "I ain't done nothing to you."

"Why did you kill that boy, Tibbs? And why did you shoot Harry?"

"You shot harry?" called out one of the patrons.

"Harry brung that kid down to the Rose Petal, figuring I wouldn't know, 'cause I was here. Well, I seen him and that kid leave, and I figured sneak, Harry was up to no good, so I followed them."

"Why did you shoot the boy?" demanded Clay.

"Cause I caught him fucking Lu Wong. She's my woman. I told him I'd show him."

"She's not your woman. No one can own a woman. You might be able to rent that one for a short while, but you don't own her. You're like a wild animal, Tibbs. A wild rabid skunk." And clay brought the barrel of the shot gun up level with Tibbs mid-section. They were fifteen feet apart.

"You gotta' be fair. You gotta' give me a chance."

"Sure, I'll give you the same chance you gave young Zach", and he raised the shotgun up to his shoulder to a firing position.

Tibbs moved along the back wall of the bar room like a trapped animal. He finally realized that it was either do or die, and he reached for his pistol.

Clay shot Tibbs in the mid-section and splattered him against the back wall. Then Clay quickly swung the shotgun around the room, looking for anyone who might be ready to draw. No one moved.

One of the patrons spoke up, "No one coming at you, mister. You done what you came for, and I recon' he had it coming. Tibbs was a menace to us all. Go in peace."

There were murmurs of "yeah" from the rest of the patrons. Clay pulled the shotgun down to his side, turned and left the saloon.

As Clay entered the store, Megan and Remy looked up. They let out a deep sigh of relief at seeing that he was safe, and yet they were anxious to know about Tibbs.

"Tibbs went for his gun and I shot him. He is gone to glory. No one interfered and, in fact, I think the other patrons were glad to see Tibbs gone."

"Remy?" Clay tone and expression were begging to know how they were doing.

Remy looked toward Megan and said, "She's holding her mud together, Clay. It's going to take a while. I'm doing fine."

Megan spoke up. "Clay, I'm sorry you had to do that. I'm sure it isn't an easy thing to just shoot a man, even if it is in self-defense. Poor Harry. He meant well for everyone. He just wasn't aware of how the world was spinning around him. And Zach? I think that he just became a lost soul, letting his urges out that he had held in for so long. I don't blame him for what happened between us. It just happened. I am so sorry for him, sorry that his life ended so violently and so young. It's still going to be a while for me to process all this and feel grounded."

"Remy placed his hand on Megan's and said, "You take all the time you need. Just remember that I'm here to help in whatever way you need.

Megan looked back at Remy. She had a curious look on her face, as if she was wondering about what he meant by what he said.

Clay seemed to sense how she was reacting. It was as if Remy was going to allow her the time to settle her mind about Zach's sudden departure, as if she was beholden to Remy to get clear and be herself again, whatever that was. However, Clay knew that however she reconciled all that had happened and was yet to happen in

Bodie and between her and Zach, it would be for her sake, and her alone. Not in any way to satisfy Remy.

Megan looked to Clay and he gave her a knowing look and slight nod in return.

From their first meeting, Megan had felt that she and Clay shared a special bond, a bond of mutual empathy.

After an hour or so had passed, and no one had said anything. Remy suggested that they go up to the undertaker's, if Megan felt up to it.

"I'm okay. That's a good idea. I'll grab a fresh change of clothes for him just in case they need it."

As they walked outside, Clay saw Molly McGuire walking toward him, and she waved to him when he looked up. He turned to Remy and Megan and told them to walk on ahead slowly, and he walked over to meet Molly McGuire.

"Molly, are you coming to see me?"

"I am, young man. I've got some news for you that might be good, or not."

"And what would that news be, Molly?"

A group of us just returned from Bridgeport. We went up there to fetch two wagon loads of supplies for all of us. We just got back. On our way back, I noticed two men camped down by the creek, about two miles back. Seemed odd to me because they was just sitting there, and there is nothing there to do, and then I remembered that you was expecting two men to come here after that Barnes couple. Sorry to hear about Zach and Harry. Anyway, I thought you would want to know about them two.

"Thanks, Molly. They might be the ones, and I hope that they are. I want to get that matter settled as soon as we can. If they are camped that close, it means that they will be coming into town either tonight or at first light tomorrow.

"You want any help?"

"No thanks, Molly. I think that Remy Jones and I can handle it okay. You keep out of harm's way."

Clay thanked Molly again, and bid her good day. He quickly caught up with Remy and Megan.

They walked the few blocks to Stokes' undertaker parlor. Stokes greeted them and took them in the back room where he had the coffins in which he had placed Zach and Harry.

Megan held out the clothes she brought for Zach. "Here, Mr. Stakes. In case you need these for Zach."

"No thanks, ma'am. I picked up the young man's clothes at the scene, and they fit fine."

"Weren't his clothes bloody from being shot? Megan asked.

"No ma'am, he wasn't wearing any clothes when he was shot or when he was thrown out the window. His clothes was tossed down afterwards. They was clean."

Megan was surprised, and a few tears appeared in her eyes, but she quickly wiped them and looked down.

"I got them already them in the coffins, and I got several open graves already dug at the cemetery. We could bury them first thing in the morning, if you like."

"We might as well," replied Megan. What time?"

"Should be early, ma'am, before it warms up, say about nine o'clock?"

"Okay, Mr. Stokes, how much do we owe you for all this?"

Well, ma'am, young Zach had $12 in his pocket, and that would be enough for him. Supposed I just say that however much money Harry had in his pockets will cover his cost?"

"Fine, Mr. Stokes. Thank you again."

As the three started to leave Stokes' place, Clay asked the other two to wait for him outside for a moment. He wanted to speak to Stokes. They nodded and walked out the door, closing it behind them.

"Mr. Stokes, I wanted to speak to you about some business that might be coming your way soon."

"Yes, sir. What would that be about?"

"There are two men coming to town, either tonight or tomorrow morning. They're coming after me and the Barnes couple, although it's just Megan now that Zach is dead. However, they don't know about that. Remy and I will be ready to greet them, and I can assure you that whichever way the coin falls, two of the four of us are going to end up dead. You might want to get two more coffins ready. You can have whatever you find on them, along with their guns. We're taking their horses and saddles, however. If they come in the morning, we might have to delay the Barnes funeral, but it won't belong. And there won't be anyone coming to bury these other two guys."

"Thanks for the tip, Mr. Jameson. I just might be ready. And you might just want to stay around Bodie. You'd be good for my business."

"Yeah, thanks, but I don't think so."

Clay joined the other and they walked back toward the store. He relayed what Molly had told him. It made them breathe a little easier for now, and allowed them the time to time to prepare for tomorrow.

They were nearing the store, when all of a sudden Megan stopped, turned to Clay and said, "Clay, I need a favor. From you too, Remy."

'Well, sure, Megan. Just name it."

This might seem a little strange to you, but I want to speak to Lu Wong."

Clay and Remy looked at Megan, and then at each other. They were startled, to say the least.

"And what might you want to see Lu Wong about," asked Clay. He immediately got suspicious and thought Megan might want some sort of revenge on Lu Wong.

"It's a private matter. I'm not going to hurt her, if that's what you think. I just need to ask her something."

"I'm not so sure that she will want to see you, Megan. It might to seem strange to her, given the circumstance."

"I know, but I have to try. Will you two take me there?"

"Sure, Megan. Let's go now, while you're in the mood. Who knows what tomorrow will bring?"

And they walked up the street and over to Chinatown and stopped at the Rose Pearl. Megan moved forward and opened the door, and Clay and Remy followed.

They were greeted by the old man, Ben. He had a surprised look on his face, and asked, "Good afternoon. How may Ben help you?" and he looked back and forth at their faces trying to determine which one would answer.

"I'm Megan Barnes, Ben, my husband was the man shot and thrown out of the window earlier today.

"Yes, Mrs. Barnes. I know who you are. But why are you here. There is nothing we can do for you here."

"Yes, there is, Ben. I'm not here to cause any trouble. I know what happened was not the fault of anyone here. However, I need to speak to Lu Wong, just for a few minutes.'

"I'm sorry Mrs. Barnes. I don't think she is here right now."

"It's okay, Ben," came a voice from the railing upstairs. "I'll speak with the lady." And Lu Wong proceeded to walk down the stairs and walk up to Megan.

"I am very sorry for your loss, Mrs. Barnes. That's all I can say."

"Thank you, Lu Wong. I know it was not your fault. Is there somewhere private where I may speak with you for just a few minutes?"

Lu Wong was silent. She wasn't sure what Megan might have in mind.

She watched Megan's face and saw the serious expression and felt the real concern that this woman had. Lu Wong sensed that it took an incredible amount of nerve for Megan to swallow her pride and put aside any anger or blame she must have had for Lu Wong to face her like this. Finally, she said, "we can go into Ben's office room right here," and she pointed to the door leading to the front office.

"But Lu Wong, are you sure," Ben started to ask.

"It's okay, Ben. Mrs. Barnes and I will speak.

Lu Wong led Megan into Ben's office. One of Lu Wong's co-workers, Soo Chen, was in there. "You want me go?" asked Soo Chen.

"No," responded Megan. It might be even better if she stays and I can ask her too." Megan shut the door.

They were in there for what seemed for a long time. Ben knocked on the door once and asked if everything was alright, and he was assured by Lu Wong that they were fine. Occasionally there were giggles coming from the room. Remy and Clay just looked at each other and shrugged their shoulders.

The door opened after about twenty minutes and the two women walked out, smiling and holding hands.

"Megan turned to Clay and Remy and asked, "Are you guys ready?" and then he turned back to Lu Wong, and said, "Thank you so very much, Lu Wong. I know that you must have wondered what on earth I might want to ask, but when I did ask, you were very kind and understanding. And you are a wise woman, Lu Wong. I hope that I can be so wise. Please thank Soo Chen for me."

Megan led the way out the door and back toward the store. Remy and Clay were stupefied, and they shrugged their shoulders and joined Megan. Neither of them dared ask about the conversation between Megan and Lu Wong until then neared the store.

Clay finally had to know and he asked, "You gals were in there for a long time. What was that all about?"

"I was learning about the mysteries of life." And that was all she would say.

They each hoped that someday Megan would confide in them, and they agreed to tell each other if Megan told any one of them.

Back at the store, Megan prepared supper, while Clay and Remy worked out their sleeping arrangements. Clay expected the night to get very cold so he took two extra blankets out to his bed in the livery area.

No one said much during the evening. They were caught up in their own thoughts. Megan knew that she was going back home and she ran a number of scenarios through her mind, trying to sort out how she wanted her return to go. Several times she glanced at Remy and at Clay, as if trying to make up her mind.

She expected Remy to propose to her soon in some fashion, but she didn't know what to expect from Clay. He wasn't the marrying type, she had concluded. Nevertheless, he was very appealing in all his manhood. But he was his own man, and would not necessarily follow her lead. Remy was the more moldable type; more willing to take directions than to give them. She thought that her father would easily take to Remy, and that could eventually lead to her running the business for her father. Something will work out, she mused. It always does.

Remy glanced often at Megan and imagined the various approaches he could take to ask to accompany her home, with the idea of asking her father's permission to marry her. He wanted that to go well.   He planned on helping Clay tomorrow take on Scully and Rand, but he also planned on being carefully not to take a bullet himself

Clay mentally worked out several ways to take on Scully and Rand. He was glad for Remy's help, but he never counted on anything for sure. He figured on taking Rand first because Rand was more the cold gunslinger type and would be less anxious to face another man's gun.

After supper, they engaged some in small talk. Megan gathered up her personal belongings and packed most of them in three boxes. Clay cleaned and oiled his Winchester and his Colt, and made certain that he had enough cartridges. Remy moved his sleeping quarters from the Inn to the front of the store, and stared out the window.

It was about 4:00 a.m. when Scully woke Rand, "It's time to go."

"I'd sure like some coffee, John. I could build a small fire. It wouldn't take long."

"No time for coffee, Rand. We gotta' get there before first light. I'll tell you what, I expect the saloons in Bodie to open by 6:00 a.m., to catch the morning shift on their way to work and the night shift on their home. We'll stop at the first saloon we find open, have us drink, and learn what we can about that Barnes couple. You can get your coffee there too, if you'd rather have coffee than whiskey."

"Whiskey sound just fine, John. Something to warm my bones. I'm frozen clear through."

They saddled their horses and tied their bed rolls on the back, and rode off toward Bodie. The sky was clear and full of stars. It was mid-July, with a new moon and it wouldn't be full 'til about the end of the month.

Chapter 14

Given the nature of events that had occurred, Clay suggested that both he and Remy sleep at the store. They could make up some sort of bed out of some blankets and pillows that Megan had. Clay went over to Molly McGuire's livery and picked up his gear. Remy did the same at his hotel.

Clay asked Remy to make up a bed in the front of the store, while Clay planned to sleep out in the small livery stable that Harry had built. That way they would have coverage on the entrances to the store. Remy didn't object. He much preferred sleeping inside rather than out in that cold night air; and it does get cold at night in Bodie.

"How do you want to handle things in the morning, Clay?" asked Remy.

"Well, we're not sure how they're coming into town. I say we get up early and each take a side of the street, and play it by ear. Megan will lock both doors and stay inside, but out of sight. Do you have any better suggestions?"

"No. Sounds good to me. Like you say, we don't know exactly what to expect, but we can handle whatever comes."

"Clay asked Megan, "What are your plans for tomorrow, after we are clear of Scully and Rand?"

"I'm leaving here as soon as possible and going back home. I was looking forward to your company on the way, if you are ready to leave too."

"And I am looking forward to accompanying you." They looked at each other and shared a smile. "We'll be finished here soon, and none too soon for me. Nothing has gone as expected and so far, and we have had some tragic experiences."

"You're right, of course, Clay, but not all the experiences have been bad. I feel that I have learned a great deal in just a short time, and that I am a different person now than I was when Zach and I first started for Bodie."

Remy was listening and finally offered a comment, "I was planning to accompany you too, Megan."

"And I was planning on that, Remy," said Megan. "When the time is right, we need to talk about a few things, you and me."

That comment made Remy feel good. She seemed to know his intentions and if he didn't ask for her hand soon, he thought that she will do it for him. She seemed more self-confident and certainly more assertive than even this morning.

Clay rose, picked up his Winchester and said, "Well, good night you two. Sleep fast. We have a big day tomorrow. Don't let any stranger in, and lock the door behind me."

"Good night, Clay." Responded Megan

"Catch you early tomorrow, Clay, Remy said.

"Oh, and by the way, Megan. I'm leaving my shotgun right here on the counter. It's loaded, pointed at the front door, and ready to fire. If one of those guys comes in that way, just pull the trigger.'

"With pleasure," replied Megan.

"But just be sure that I'm not in the way, said Remy. "Remember that I'm over this way." And he pointed to his bedroll.

Clay laughed and then went out to Harry's livery and settled in for the night, as much as any of them would settle in this night.

A little before 6:00 a.m., Scully and Rand walked their horses into Bodie. They had initially ridden half way around the town and were coming the side door, as it were. They noticed that the lights were burning inside one of the saloons on the main street, up a few doors from a livery stable.

"Scully said, "Will put the horses up there, at the livery, and have them feed and water them. They'll be already for travel when we need them."

"Okay, John."

They walked their horses around back of the stable and dismounted. They were met by a crusty old woman who asked, "What do you men want?"

"Just feed and water them. They might need a rub down too. We'll be back later today. Might stay a night or not. It all depends." And they walked around to the street and up to the saloon called Rondo's.

"What will it be gentlemen?" asked Rondo.

"I'll have a whiskey, make it a double." Said Scully.

"I'll have the same and a cup of coffee, if you have it ready."

"Coming up," said Rondo.

Rondo brought their drinks and said, "You fellas must be new in town. It don't look like you're going to work or coming from work."

"Is that a problem?" Growled Scully.

"No. Not a problem. Just making conversation. You see, most people coming in at this time are either going to work and need a bracer or they are coming home from work and need a relaxer. I get 'em either way." And Rondo laughed at his own comments.

"Anything happening in this town?" asked Scully.

"Just the usual shootings," said Rondo. "Had three shot yesterday afternoon."

"You don't say." Said Scully. "Who got shot?"

"Fella that owned a store just down the street and around the corner. He and his nephew both shot within a few minutes of each other, and then the shooter got shot by a friend of the nephew. Shot him right back there." And the bartender pointed to the rear of the saloon.

"You don't say," responded Scully.

"So, what happened to the friend?"

"Oh nothing. The guy he shot was a no-good bully, and everyone is glad to be rid of him."

"So where did the friend go?"

"He's probably down at the store with the nephew' wife; pretty young thing, she is. Too young to be a widow."

The bartender moved down the bar to wait on new customers.

"Well can you beat that, "commented Scully. Some bad ass has done half our work for us. All we got to do is take the girl, and kill that Jameson character in the process."

"Yeah, and if they're both in the store, we got them cornered. Let's go get 'em now, John. Then we can take the girl and get out of here. This town gives me the creeps."

"Finish your drink and we'll go. When they got outside of the saloon, Scully said to Rand, "you walk down and around the corner and get near the store's front door. I'll cut across the lot next to the livery and come up behind the store. I'll shoot into the door as a distraction. When you hear me shoot, you smash in the front door of the store and go in shooting. But don't hit the girl."

Rand walked around to the front of the store while Scull walked quietly across the lot and headed for the back of the store. As he approached the store, he saw Jameson coming out of Harry's livery and Jameson didn't see him. What luck. He drew his gun, leveled it at Jameson, and said "Don't move or I'll shoot you dead where you stand."

Scull had thought quickly, and instead of shooting Jameson as soon as he saw him, he thought to use him to make the girl open the door to the store. Then he would shoot him, and their work was done.

Jameson stood motionless, knowing that Scull would shoot and couldn't miss from this distance. Why had he been so careless as to get caught so easily?

Scully walked closer to Jameson. "Now lift your pistol slowly by your thumb and finger and drop it on the ground. My gun is cocked and aimed right at your belly, so don't be a hero. I'll kill you before you can clear leather."

Clay decided to do what Scully asked and stall for time, so he reached for his gun with two fingers and started to lift it from the holster. Then he heard the crack of a rifle shot coming somewhere toward the back of the lot. Scully let out a groan and arched his back in pain. The gun fell out of his hand.

Clay didn't take time to think about what had happened, he just drew his pistol with a full hand and shot Scully twice before he hit the ground. Jameson looked toward the location where the rifle shot came from and he saw Molly McGuire, big as life, waiving to him. She had a rifle in her hand. He waived in return. What a woman, *he mused.*

As Clay was waiving to Molly, several pistol shots rang out, coming from in front of the store, and then came the unmistakable sound of a shotgun blast.

Clay ran to the back door and tried to open it. It was locked. He smashed one of the door windows and reached around and turned the handle, opened the door and rushed in. Megan was standing behind the counter, holding her hands to her face. The shotgun lay on the counter in front of her. Remy was standing near the front door, looking down at a body. Rand lay dead in the doorway.

Megan grabbed hold of Clay in a big hug. She let out a few sobs of relief. It was over. She was free.

Remy and Clay gave each other a quick salute, acknowledging their triumph. Remy took hold of Rand by the shirt collar and dragged his body into the side of the street. They knew that Stokes would be along shortly with his dead body wagon. And he was. He said he would meet them at the cemetery at ten o'clock.

"Remy," Said Clay, why don't you harness up Megan's wagon. Her horses are in Harry's livery," and clay pointed out the back door, "I have to go over the McGuire's livery and thank Molly. I owe her a lot. I'll explain later.

Remy nodded his agreement. Clay walked over to see Molly. She had walked half way to the store and they greeted each other with grins and hugs.

"Molly, I owe you my life, and I'm in your debt forever. Nice shooting, by the way,"

"Shucks, Clay. You don't owe me anything. I was glad for the opportunity to try out the old rifle," She was grinning from ear to ear, like she had really enjoyed the event.

"How did you know it was Scully?"

"Clay, "she explained, "Those two guys left their horses at our livery. That's how I knew they was here and I kept my eye on them. They went to the saloon and then headed back, but they split up and headed for the store, in different directions. I knew that they was up to no good.

When I saw that he was making you give up your gun, I knew I had to act, so I took careful aim, so as not to hit you, and I shot him, POW, just like that. And boy, did it ever feel good."

"I'm glad you enjoyed it. Those kind of opportunities don't come along very often," and they laughed at the situation.

"Say, Clay, those two horses they left might belong to Megan's father. Check the brand and see if you recognize it." Clay did and yes, they wore the Williams brand.

"Molly, which do you think is the better horse?"

"I think the bay gelding is the better one by far."

"That's what I thought too, Molly. I'm taking the other one, the roan, back with us. The bay is yours. That's the least I could do."

"Why thank you, Clay. I'll take good care of him. I hope you come back this way again someday. You've provided some welcome excitement these past two days.'

"Thanks, Molly. You're a true friend and all women, but I think I have been Bodied out, if you know what I mean."

"When will you heading out?"

"Right after the funeral for Harry, after ten o'clock."

Remy started out the back door to hitch the horses to the wagon, but stopped and turned to Megan. "Megan, we don't' have much time now for small talk so I'll get right to the point. I love you, Megan, but you already know that. I want to go home with you and asks your father for his permission for your hand in marriage. We should do this proper."

Megan stood there staring at Remy for the longest minute, and Remy began to wonder what her reaction would be. Maybe he had rushed things too much.

Finally, Megan's face broke into a broad smile, and she went to Remy and engaged him is a long and full kiss. I was beginning to think you weren't going to ask. I love you too, Remy. Should we tell Clay?

"We won't half to. I think he already knows. If not, he'll figure it out before we get too far.

Remy had the horses hitched to the wagon and he and Megan had begun to load their personal belongings. Clay saddled and led the roan horse over to Remy and said, "here, courtesy of Megan's father. It's got his brand on it. We'll tie him on to the back of the wagon, and you can take him when we get home.

"Well thank you, Clay. Did this belong to Scully or Rand?"

'I think that was the one Scully was riding." Clay figured that by saying that, Remy would feel that he got the better of the two horses.

"I think that we're all loaded and ready to go," said Megan. You guys ready?"

"What about the rest of the merchandise in the store? Asked Remy.

"I took what I wanted and got enough food and other things we'll need for the trip home. Whoever want it can have it. I'm through with this place for ever."

They drove up to the cemetery, with Remy driving the wagon and Megan sitting at his side. Clay's blue dun mare was fresh and ready to run.

Stokes had both caskets laying alongside their respective graves. He had had the sites marked with hand-made crosses that had their names carved in them. Only their date of death was shown.

They all stood there for a few moments, and then Stokes asked if anyone wanted to say anything. Remy and Clay both looked at Megan.

"Well, Zach, you had a short life," began Megan.

Too short for anyone, and I'm sorry. If your mother is right, then you've gone to the Lord. If she's not, then you're going to be in this grave for a long time." Then Megan looked at Clay and then at Remy and said, "You know, I fell in love with the boy, but I never knew the man. I don't think that I would have like him."

"Uncle Harry," continued Megan, "it was you who got us here, and in a way, it's you who is letting us go. I feel that I came here as a girl and I am leaving here as a woman. I thank you for that."

Several of the townsfolk had come to the funeral: Patrick and Molly McGuire, and four or five people that they didn't know. Molly turned to them and said, "Folks I want to thank you for coming. I appreciate your consideration. We are leaving this town in about five minutes and I am leaving the store and its merchandise to whomever wants it. Help yourselves.

Megan turned to Clay and Remy and said, "Shall we go gentlemen."

Chapter 15

The trip home was uneventful. Hot days and cold nights, and lots of dust in between.

It was eventful, however, when one considers how the relationship between Megan and Remy developed. On the first night, the three of them made camp in a grove of Aspen and Cottonwood trees, next to a stream a few miles north of Bridgeport. The day had been hot and dry, and the horses were exhausted. So were the three of them.

They had brought along a small tent from Harry's store for Megan to use. Clay and Remy slept under the stars, or in Clay's case, under the wagon. In the middle of the night, Remy quietly slipped out of bedroll and just as quietly slipped into Megan's tent. She was awake, as if expecting him. She opened her bedroll and Remy crawled in next to her. She placed her hands on his face and felt it all over, as if she was looking for something.

"My face hasn't changed," said Remy.

"I know," Megan replied. "But it makes it more intimate for me to feel your face before me. I was hoping you would come, but I wasn't sure that you would.

We're traveling beyond the bounds of propriety, you know,"

"Yes, I know," Remy acknowledged, and they kissed long and hard. "And I'm loving the trip."

They made love, or as Megan admitted later, they just had sex, and it was good sex.

Later, after their love-making, Megan told Remy that this would be it until they were married. She enjoyed the sex and had no regrets, but she had been thinking since about everything they had been through all the implications, including the feelings of her parents and Zach's parents. She just had to pull back and be a little more reserved going forward.

Remy said that he understood completely. He told her that didn't want to pressure her and that he could wait until she was ready. He also wanted to get her father's blessing.

Megan felt unsettled by his reaction. This was the third time that he was able to turn the situation around and make it about himself. She didn't need his approval nor his understanding for how she felt. It wasn't about him. This was on her.

No more was said about it by either of them, and Clay seemed either not to know or not to care what had occurred between them because he said nothing. Actually, he felt a little sad. That was an odd feeling. Was he sad that Megan had given herself to someone other than him? Probably! Or was he sad because he had strong feelings for her and didn't tell her how he felt? Probably! However, he was not about to get tangled in the affairs of the Williams family, and he did not want to marry anyone, Not yet He just wasn't ready to settle down.

They were about two days from home when Clay said that he would ride on ahead. He could make better time on horseback than they did in the wagon, and he would prepare those at home for their arrival.

Clay asked both of them, "Am I correct in assuming that the two of you plan to marry?"

"You are correct," responded Remy. He puffed up a little with pride. "I plan to ask her father for her hand. I think that will make it easier on Megan."

"That's what I figured," Clay said.

"Megan asked, "What are you planning to tell my parents and Zach's parents about what happened in Bodie?"

"I think we need am explanation that we can all agree to and use when anyone asks, "responded Clay.

"How does this sound," offered Remy: *About mid-day on last Wednesday, people heard some shooting right* in the *middle of town. They ran out and found both Harry and Zach lying in the street, dead. They had been shot by a deranged miner, who was seen running into a local saloon after the shooting. After we saw to the bodies, Clay went to the saloon and confronted the man. He threatened to shoot Clay, as well, and drew his pistol. Clay out drew him and shot the man. Because of the heat and the distance from any larger town, they all had to be buried quickly. Zach and Harry were buried in the local cemetery, with markers of wood. The killer was buried in boot hill.*

"That's a great rendition, responded Clay. I like to add that *both Scully and Rand were killed by local residents when they tried to storm the store.*

Megan and Remy agreed, and that was to be their story.

Remy asked, "How are you going to explain the fact of coming ahead alone and leaving Megan and me to travel together?"

Megan responded, "Say that it was my idea. That I wanted Zach's parents to learn of his death as soon as possible, and that I was escorted by a *trusted friend*."

Remy and Clay looked at Megan and then at each other, and Clay said, "That sounds good to me."

Remy agreed, although he didn't like to be thought of as just a friend.

Clay decided that he would visit Zach's parents first and explain his death as best he could. He said that he would meet them in two days at the Williams' residence.

Their stories seemed to cover all the circumstances, and there was nothing more to be said, so Clay said his goodbyes and rode away.

Clay rode alone the rest of the way to Sacramento and caught the late afternoon paddlewheel steamer at for Martinez. On the way, Clay first rubbed down his horse, fed and watered her, and then he took a stateroom so that he could wash and shave.

Afterward, he fell sound asleep on the bed. He had left word for the steward, or whatever the man was called, to be wakened before they landed.

The boat arrived back in Martinez at about 8:00 a.m. Clay saddled *Blue* and road the few miles to Andersville.

It was too early to call on the Williams or the Barnes, he thought, so he rode over to Consolidated Transportation to see Bill Heck.

He entered the livery at the rear of the store and was greeted there by Heck, with his welcoming open arms and his face lit up with a big grin.

"Well, Clay, my boy. Who said you died?"

"Never mind the charm, Heck." Clay dismounted, and drew the shotgun from its scabbard.

"Here's you 12-gauge, Heck. A handy tool, I must say."

"Hey," responded Heck, "there are a few dents here in the stock and it needs to be cleaned."

"Pay it no mind, my friend. Let's go buy me some breakfast and I'll relate to you the further adventures of Clay Jameson.

Clay and Bill Heck walked to a nearby restaurant, and Clay gave an account of his trip, but excluded any reference to a possible relationship between Megan and Remy. Heck listened and nodded and laughed, and grunted all at the appropriate places during Clay story.

"I'm really sorry to hear about Zach, dying the way he did. I had better hopes for that boy."

"Yes, Heck, I think everyone did."

"So where do you go from here," asked Heck.

"Well, I have to visit with the Williams family and the Barnes folks. It's going to be hard on Mrs. Barnes to lose a son like she did. I'll be able to soften it to spare her some feelings and let her believe that it was God's will. I'm not sure how it will go with Mr. or Mrs. Williams. That's going to be interesting."

"Is this Remy character moving in on Megan?" Asked Heck.

"I think he already has. They said that they were planning to get married. However, I have some reservations about his sincerity that I have to work out. I don't want to see Megan get hurt anymore."

"Sounds like you might be thinking about moving in on Megan yourself, you sly old fox." Heck shoved Clay gently in his arm.

"No, Heck, not me. She is a wonderful woman, but I'm too young for that sort of life. Anyway, I wouldn't be any good for her. She's a strong woman and I don't fit into her life plans."

"Meaning that you don't want to be bossed around by a woman," said Heck.

"Au contraire, mon ami," I like strong women. I just don't like them trying to run my life."

"Amen to that, rejoined Heck.

Clay shoved his empty breakfast plate forward and rose from his chair. "Thanks for the breakfast, Heck. I'm going over to see Mr. and Mrs. Barnes, then to see Mr. Williams. If it's alright with you, I'd like to stay at your place another night or two. I'm going to meet Megan and Remy and see how that works out with the Williams family."

"Sure, Clay. See you later."

Clay visited with Mr. and Mrs. Barnes and tried to explain Zach's death as he, Remy and Megan had agreed upon, but without all the negative details. The Barnes couple seemed to age before Clay's eyes at the news. They just sat in those rocker on the front porch and cried. Clay excused himself and left. He could do no more.

Next, Clay went to Mr. Williams' office. There was a sign on the door saying, *Closed due to illness*. Then he rode over to the Williams' home. It was large house built of think timbers and stone, surrounded by a hand-made rail fence, and it had a large archway over the entrance gate. Mrs. Williams answered the door when Clay knocked.

"Yes, may I help you?"

"Yes, Mrs. Williams, my name is Clay Jameson. Hour husband hired me to..."

"I know who you are, Mr. Jameson. My husband explained it all to me. Won't you come? I supposed you've come to give us a report?"

"Yes, I have, as a matter of fact. Is Mr. Williams at home? I saw the closed sign on his office door. Nothing serious, I trust?"

Chapter 16

Mr. Williams is not doing very well. Shortly after you left, he came down with a cold, and it kept getting worse. Finally, the doctor made him go to bed and get some rest. Now the doctor thinks that the cold has moved it to pneumonia. He's prescribed some medication, but Mr. Williams is not responding. I don't know…" and she let her voice trail off.

"I'm sorry to hear that, Mrs. Williams. May I talk to him? I know he'd want to hear my report."

"Yes, you better do that. I don't think your visit will affect him either way."

She led Clay into the bedroom, where Mr. Williams was sitting up in bed, but dozing. The room was lit by only one small kerosene lamp. The bed was a built of dark mahogany and was a massive structure.

Williams looked up when he heard them enter and asked, "Who's that?"

"It's me, Mr. Williams, Clay Jameson."

"Well, it's about time young man." And Williams perked up and opened his eyes wide. "You've come to report, I take it."

"Yes, if you are up to it."

"I'm fine. This damn doctor won't let me go to work until I get rid of this rattle in my chest. So, they tell me."

Clay looked over at Mrs. Williams. He wasn't sure what he should say about Scully and Rand. He wasn't sure how much Mrs. Williams knew.

"Go on, tell me what happened. It's alright. She knows everything."

"First off, Megan is on her way home."

"Praise the Lord," said Williams.

"Well sir, the Lord didn't play a role in the events that transpired. Zach is dead, shot by a drunken man in the streets of Bodie. Harry went to help him and he was shot as well. I followed the man into a local saloon and called him out. He went for his gun, but I drew first and shot him. Zach and Harry are buried next to each other in the Bodie cemetery.

"Oh, my God," said Mrs. Williams. "How horrible. Mrs. Barnes will be so shocked. How is Megan taking it?"

"Megan is taking it very well. As a matter of fact,

their marriage wasn't working out very well. I think that they would have separated anyway."

Mr. Williams spoke up, "Sounds as if things worked out the way I wanted them to without you or my two men having to lift a finger. I told...."

"Don't say it, Mr. Williams." Interrupted Clay.

"Don't say what?"

"Don't say *I told you so*. When you see Megan, don't say that. That's the last remark she wants to hear. Her experience was difficult enough without you rubbing it in."

"Okay, I won't. So where are my two ranch hands? Did you see them?

"Yes, Mr. Williams. I saw them. They tried to raid Harry's store to get Megan, but it didn't work well for them. I shot Scully full of little holes and another local resident shot Rand. They're dead, Mr. Williams. Gone to glory. No thanks to you." Clay's tone lay somewhere between humorous and sarcastic.

"Wait a minute, Mr. Jameson," queried Mrs. Williams. "You said that Megan was coming home and yet you are here. Where is she now?"

"We traveled together with our mutual friend from Bodie until yesterday. They're coming home in the wagon. I rode on ahead."

"That don't sound right, Jameson," said Mr. Williams. Who is this mutual friend?"

"He is a young man named Remington Jones, Remy he's called. He was working as a mining engineer for some of the local mines. His work was finish and he was preparing to leave, when Zach and Megan showed up. He delayed his plans and was helping them and Harry unload their supplies and then he was helping Harry and Zach with the store.

Mrs. Williams interrupted and said, "You mean to tell me that she is out there now, along with a perfect stranger,"

"Well, Mrs. Williams, I don't think he's perfect, and he is not a stranger, not any longer. He is a very nice, responsible and honest man, and I'm sure that he would not take advantage of the situation. Of course, that's not the point, is it?"

"What do you mean?" Mrs. Williams was speaking with a harsher tone now.

"I mean that Megan is a mature, self-assured, and responsible person, and she is in charge of the situation, not him. Give her the credit that she is due, something that you, Mr. Williams have been reluctant to do.

"Don't tell me what to do with my daughter." Grumbled Mr. Williams.

"Well, someone has to. Are you still that demanding and unforgiving man I found when I first met you?"

"I am, Mr. Jameson, but you always have a way of tempering that side of me."

"Try tempering it yourself, sometime, Mr. Williams. You'd be surprised how much more receptive that people will be of you."

Clay continued, "And I must tell both of you that Remy is now more than a friend. I don't know if you two can remember what love is like, but it is an elusive spirit that one cannot control. Apparently, Remy and Megan are in love, and he is planning to ask you, Mr. Williams, for your permission to marry Megan."

"Gracious sakes, Mr. Jameson," said Mrs. Williams. "This is all moving too fast for me. Give me some time to digest what you're telling me."

"That's the second piece of good news you brought me, Mr. Jameson," said Mr. Williams "Things just might work out after all. I'm dying to meet this boy."

Clay looked down at Mr. Williams and thought you might not realize it, but you don't look or sound well. You might really be dying.

Clay looked at Mrs. Williams. She looked dejected and helpless. Her husband had always controlled what they did as a couple, and probably how they felt. Now, she was at a loss without his strength and direction. Hopefully, Megan will step in and offer strength and not pity.

If you folks will excuse me, now, I need to get cleaned up. And you, Mr. Williams, need to rest. I expect Megan and Remy to be on the morning steamer about 8:00 a.m. tomorrow. I'll meet them and we'll come back here together.

Clay stopped thought for a few seconds and then turned around to address the Williams again. "I told you that Megan and Remy are planning to marry, but that he will be asking your permission to do so before any official courting begins."

"Yes, you said that. So..?" replied Mr. Williams.

'I'm sorry to mention this, but I am suspicious by nature. I don't want to say anything against Remy, but I do want Megan to be sure."

'Well, of course. So, do we" said Mrs. Williams."

"I have an idea that might prove useful in satisfying my suspicions, but I need your help.'

"Whatever it takes at this point," said Mr. Williams.

Clay explained to both of them what he had in mind and they agreed that it was a good idea and that they would help carry it out.

Clay rode back to Consolidated Transportation, and left *Blue* with one of Heck' men who promised to rub him down and feed him well. Heck had a large tub sitting just outside the tack room where Clay was to sleep. He had also heated a large pan of water on the forge used in shaping horseshoes and wagon bands. He handed clay a towel and when Clay was ready, he filled the tub with both hot and cold water until it was just the right bathing temperature.

Clay washed off the trail dust and then soaked until the water began to cool off. He got out of the tub and dried, then put on his pants and boots. Then he shaved, using a straight razor that Heck had recently honed.

. That evening, Clay and Heck walked up the street to the Anders Saloon. Clay ordered a beer with a rye chaser and Heck ordered a beer.

"Are you still drinking that rot gut with your beer," asked Heck.

"Sure. That rye ages the beer three years and gives it depth. Want to try some?"

"Not a chance. I'll stick to my beer, thank you.

They shared a little small talk and Heck filled Clay in on the fat that Williams' office had been closed for at least a week, and that folks say that he is dying of nastiness.

Clay was up early and was waiting at the ferry dock when the boat docked. Sure enough, Megan and Remy came off the boat in their wagon to greet him. Remy looked like he had cleaned up as best as he could and shaved for the occasion.

"Well, I see you made it." Said Clay. I was afraid you two might run off to the hills and I'd never see you again."

"We're here with bells on." responded Remy.

"I'd like to get home as soon as possible now and see my mother before my father gets home."

"I tried to clean up some, but I really need a bath and a descent shave before I meet Megan's parents so you go on ahead, Megan, and I'll come over later today."

"Sorry, Megan, but that's not going to happen." Said Clay. "Your father has been home in bed for over a week. He caught a cold that worked its way into pneumonia. He doesn't look very well. I think that you both should go and now and see him if just to say be welcomed home. Remy you could introduce yourself and then take you leave."

"I think Clay is right, Remy. It would be best, "said Megan.

"Alright, if you think so, Megan. Let's go, replied Remy.

They road to the Williams house and stopped the wagon in front of the door and got down. One of the ranch-hands was there and took charge of the wagon. He said they could unload it later.

Megan's mother rushed out the front door and hugged Megan like the long-lost soul she was, at least to her.

"Mom, this is Remington Jones. I supposed that Clay has filled you in on much of our ordeal, and that Remy has been a great help to us all."

"Pleasure to meet you Mr. Jones."

"Please call me Remy."

"Alright, Remy it is. Come on in. Your father is waiting to see you.

They entered the bedroom. Mr. Williams was sitting up as straight as he could. His thinning hair was combed and he was smiling.

Megan went to him and they hugged, and he kissed her on the cheek. "I'm so glad your home, Megan. We'll talk about everything a little later. Right now, I want to meet your beau.'

"Father, this is Remy Jones."

"Mr. Williams, it is a pleasure to meet you."

"My pleasure as well, Remy."

"Megan, learning that you were coming home was such good news, but we have had even more good news." Said Mrs. Williams. Your brother, Hugh, wired us last week. He is on his way home to stay for good. And he wants to help run the business. Isn't that wonderful, Megan?"

Both Mr. and Mrs. Williams had big smiles on their faces, and they looked thrilled.

Megan was taken aback. This went against all she

had thought of and expected when she decided to come home. Why is Hugh coming home now? She couldn't even remember what he looked like. Why couldn't he stay away forever? She tried not to show her disappointment.

Remy was quiet. Then he nodded to Megan and said." I should be going. I'll get cleaned up and be back later today."

"Yes, alright, Remy. She walked him to the door and out to his horse that had been tied to the wagon.

Remy took his bedroll and a bag with his clothes and personal items in it and tied it to the saddle horn. "I'll see you later, Megan."

"Remy, you are coming back, aren't you?"

Megan was filled with sudden doubts. She had expected to one day take over the business. Or, better yet, Remy could take it over after they were married. Now there was no place for him and she was no sure which direction her life would now go.

"Sure, Megan. Of course." Remy replied, but his tone was half-hearted and he hesitated looking Megan in the eye.

Clay had remained silent during the entire visit and now just said, "I'll be back later, Megan. I'll help Remy find a place to clean up and rest."

Clay and Remy road off toward town. Clay looked back and saw Megan standing there watching them go. Clay was smiling.

Remy looked at Clay and was surprised to see him smiling. "I haven't seen you smile much, Clay. You know that when you do smile a small scar across your left cheek appears. Why haven't I noticed that before?"

"I don't know, I guess it's because I don't smile often. Now I'm going to be self-conscious about smiling." And they both laughed.

"You're probably going to be living in town for a while," said Clay. "The Anders Hotel in the best for the money. Clean and no noises from the street."

"Thanks, Clay. I'll get a room for a week or so. Where will you be?"

"I'll spend tonight in town at a friend's place and go back to my office in Oakland in the morning. Megan has my address. Keep in touch, you hear. And thanks again for all you help in Bodie."

"You bet, Clay. It's been an adventure knowing

you." Remy dismounted and tied his horse to a rail in front of the hotel, and entered the hotel, carrying his personal bag.

Clay left Remy and rode toward Heck's business a few blocks away. However, he stopped after he rounded a corner, tied his horse to a hitching post, and walked back toward the hotel. He got to the corner just in time to see Remy re-tie his bag on the saddle horn, mount up, and ride off in the direction that would take him to Martinez.

Clay looked at his watch and saw that it was about an hour before the ferry sailed back to Sacramento. He walked quickly back to his horse, mounted, and started after Remy.

When Clay reached the ferry docks, he saw Remy sitting on a bench in front of the waiting area. His horse was tied by a loading area. He dismounted and tied his horse to a rail, walked over to Remy and sat down next to him on the bench.

Remy looked over sheepishly at Clay. "I had a hunch that you would follow me. I should have been more careful."

"You're not going back, are you?"

"No, I'm not. You know how it is, Clay. Taking over the business, with Megan's help is one thing. I could put up with married life for that sort of style, but without that. What would we have?"

"You would have each other and a long life to live together doing something."

"That's not enough for me, Clay. That amounts to nothing and I've been doing nothing most of my life. No! Call me a heel, if you want, but I have other plans."

"You're a heel, Remy. You're a gutless heel, to boot. I thought you had more integrity than to string her along like you did."

"That's enough Clay. I told you where I stand and you've had your say. Now leave it at that. Go preach somewhere else. And with that, Remy got up, turned his back on Clay and walked over to his horse.

Clay watched Remy walk away, and thought, *maybe I should tell him what really happened back at the ranch. No, it will be better if he finds out later. I need to tell Megan first.*

Chapter 17

Clay rode back to the Williams ranch. What was once 2,000 acres was now down to about 300 acres, but Williams had sold much of it off lot by lot, making a fortune in the process. He still owned the waterfront, with its warehouses, ships and importing business.

Clay rode up to the front of the house, dismounted and tied *Blue* to the hitching rail. Something caught his eye and he looked up. Megan had just pulled the upstairs bedroom window curtain aside and was staring down at him. They exchanged a long look, with serious expressions on their faces.

Megan knew. She knew by the way that Clay looked up at her. She knew by the fact that he returned to the ranch so soon. Her heart sank. Remy was gone!

Megan had just dressed after taking a bath. She threw on a pair of shoes and ran down stairs and out to meet Clay. They stood there about ten feet apart, each waiting for the other to open the conversation.

Finally, Megan spoke, "Remy isn't coming back, is he, Clay?"

"No Megan, he's not."

She began to cry quietly, holding her hands to her face. Clay went to her and held her.

"Why didn't he tell me? Was he that much of a coward?"

"I have no answer for that, Megan."

"I think that deep down I expected it," she said. "He always looked at situations for his advantage in any outcome. He must have felt that he professed love would be exposed over time and he couldn't deal with that."

"Megan, there is one side of this that you didn't know about before, but now you need to know." Clay took Megan's arm and led her to the swing on the front porch. "Sit with me, here, Megan, and listen to what I have to say."

"You're making me nervous, Clay. Is there more bad news?"

"No, Megan the news is not bad. You see, I liked Remy and I appreciated his help in Bodie and he expressed his love for you and said that he was going to ask your father for permission to marry you. That just didn't ring true to me. I was nagged by the feeling that he was an opportunistic sort of guy and we had just fit into his plans."

"So where is this leading, Clay. What are you trying to tell me?"

"Your brother, Hugh isn't coming home. Your parents haven't heard from him in years. They agreed to go along with me in this as a way to test Remy. I wanted to see if Remy wanted you or the business."

"You mean you put me through all that just to satisfy you nagging feeling? You …you…" and she started hitting Clay lightly on his chest. "You wonderful man." And she reached over and kissed him and hugged him, while crying and laughing at the same time.

Then Megan took Clay face in her hands and said, "I thank you so much, Clay. I know you did it because you care. You're the only honest person I have ever experienced."

Megan found that small scar on Clay's face, and rubbed it gently. She knew it was there because she had seen it before and had asked him about it.

"I have a confession to make. On that first night we were coming home, Remy crawled into my tent, as I think you know, to make love to me. I couldn't see who it wa so I took his face in my hands and felt for this scar. I didn't find it. Remy asked why I was rubbing my hands all over his face, but, of course, I could tell him that I had hoped it was you."

"So that's what brought you and Remy together, the love-making"

"One of the many things I learned from Lu Wong in Bodie is to recognize and accept that portion of myself that she called my sexual being. It's a natural part of me. I found by being married to Zach that I enjoyed sex, and I say it was sex with Remy, not love-making. There is a difference. And now that we're on the subject, I have wondered why you never made a pass at me."

"Is that a statement, Megan or a question?"

"It's a question."

"Our conversation is getting very personal. Are you comfortable with that?

"I'm very comfortable with you Clay. We have always been able to be honest with each other. Why haven't you ever made a pass at me?"

"I have three rules about making passes at women. First, I never mix business with pleasure. I was hired to do a job and I won't let my emotional feelings toward a woman run the risk of me not doing my job. It would compromise my responsibility. Second, I won't come between a man and his wife. That gets into a dirty game from which there are no winners. And third, you are too much of a woman, with ambition, intellect, and caring for me to slow you down. You told me once that you have a destiny, Megan and I don't want to spoil that for you."

"I love you, Clay. I think that I have since the first time I saw you."

"And I love you too, Megan. You are the most beautiful person who has ever come into my life. And Idon't mean your outward physical beauty. Although you have plenty of that as well."

"You reminded me that I once said that I have a destiny." Said Megan. "What about you?"

"I have a destiny, too, although mine is not as clear as yours is, and right now our destinies won't mix well. I don't want to constrain myself anymore that I would constrain you."

"So, what's my destiny, Clay?"

"The business. Your father is not well at all and I don't expect him to live much longer. I think that your mother feels the same way. It has to be you. You are the only one here to take over the business. Imagine yourself as a pioneer woman blazing a trail for women in a man's world of business. You are needed there now."

"I have to agree with part of what you say. Heading the business would be the culmination of what I have dreamed about for many years, and yet I never thought it possible. Now that it's here, I am overwhelmed. And with my feelings for you in the mix, I'm confused as well."

"Don't be. Right now, you need to support your mother and prepare to take over the business. I would only be a distraction. We'll always have our love for each other. No matter where we are, we'll always have that."

"I may have other men in my life from time to time, Clay, but I will never marry again until I marry you. You will always be the love of my life and I will always hope that one day we will become as one."

"It's a date, Megan. I'll be there."

They hugged for perhaps the last time, and Clay rode away.

The End

Other Works by this Author

Fiction

The Searching

The Zorn Conspiracy

Non-fiction

Corrections in California: An Introduction to Probation, Institutions and Parole

Criminal Procedures in California, 5th ed.

Juvenile Procedures in California, 7th ed.

Readings in Interviewing and Counseling

Readings in Administration of Justice